Shelter

M000281853

Summer 2021

*

THE STAFF OF SHELTER OF DAYLIGHT:

MANAGING EDITOR: Tyree Campbell
WEBMASTER: H David Blalock

Cover art "Distractions" by Laura Givens
Cover design by Laura Givens

Vol. II, No.2   June 2020
Shelter of Daylight is published three times a year, on the
1st days of January, June, and October in the United States
of America by Hiraeth Publishing, P.O. Box 1248, Tularosa,
NM 88352. Copyright 2021 by Hiraeth Publishing. All
rights revert to authors and artists upon publication except
as noted in selected individual contracts. Nothing may be
reproduced in whole or in part without written permission
from the authors and artists. Any similarity between places
and persons mentioned in the fiction or semi-fiction and
real places or persons living or dead is coincidental.
Writers and artists guidelines are available online at
www.hiraethsffh.com. Guidelines are also available upon
request from Hiraeth Publishing, P.O. Box 1248, Tularosa,
NM 88352, if request is accompanied by a self-addressed
#10 envelope with a first-class US stamp. Editor: Tyree
Campbell.

The First Word from the Editor

We continue the year 2021 with more than enough doom and gloom, and I daresay we are tiring of it. Hate causes wrinkles that can only be filled by cellulite. If you wish to escape for at least a moment from surreality, here's your chance: that's what *Shelter of Daylight* is for.

At Hiraeth Publishing, we publish works on pretty much any science fiction, fantasy, or spooky horror topic or theme. *Shelter of Daylight*, however, is reserved for stories, poems, art, and articles that have an uplifting aspect to them. That's not to say you won't find danger, tension, and conflict in here. Quite the contrary. But in each piece you read, there will be something good coming out of it.

So take a moment from the rest of Existence, turn off the news and the Internet, and settle back for...adventures.

Tyree Campbell
Editor

Corporatia has quietly begun to plot against the independent world of Vanadis and enslave or kill its people. It believes the founder and protector of Vanadis, a retired assassin named Ovin Shannen, who hired out under the name of Candle, may be dead. If so, it is safe for Corporatia to move. But Shannen has spent the last few years away from his world, as a bird leads a snake away from the nest.

His teenage daughter Aisling, however, will move the stars and the corporations in her determination to bring him home. She and her twin brother steal a ship and go off among the stars to search for him, encountering perils no children should have to face. Still, she and her father have allies, including a charm quark —an energy being from another part of the galaxy. But if Aisling is to save Vanadis and bring her father home, the Fates will require sacrifices—offerings of that which must be surrendered in order to protect a loved one.

https://www.hiraethsffh.com/product-page/dog-at-war-by-tyree-campbell

A Little Help, Please

In the world of the small indie press we fight a never-ending battle for attention to our work, as writers and in publishing. Here's an example: big publishers [you know who they are] have gobs of $$$ that they can devote to advertising and marketing. Here at Hiraeth Publishing, our advertising budget consists of the deposits for whatever soda bottles and aluminum cans we can find alongside the highways. Anti-littering laws make our task even more difficult . . . ☺

That's where YOU come in. YOU are our best promoter. YOU are the one who can tell others about us. Just send 'em to our website, tell them about our store. That's all. Just that.

Of course, we don't mind if you talk us up. We're pretty good, you know. We have some award-winning and award-nominated writers and artists, plus other voices well-deserving to be heard [not everyone wins awards, right?] but our publications are read-worthy nevertheless.

That number once again is:

www.hiraethsffh.com

Friend us on Facebook at Hiraeth Publish
Follow us on Twitter at
> **@ HiraethPublish1**

Oswald's Raven
Vonnie Winslow Crist

607 A.D., York, Kingdoms of Bernica and Deira

"Oswald," said the raven as she landed beside the fair-haired toddler playing in the royal garden. At least that's what the servant woman told Queen Aacha of Bernica and Deira had happened.

"I scooped Oswald up. Brought him inside. But the bird will not leave," explained Hazel. She pointed at the bright-eyed raven perched on a chair near the young prince's bed. The frightened servant woman held her royal charge tightly against her bosom.

"It is a sign," responded Aacha with a calmness and certainty that served her well in her role as queen. Drawing her eyebrows together, the Anglo-Saxon ruler ran one of her long, yellow plaits through her fingers, then motioned for Hazel to take the prince back outside.

"Ravens travel between worlds," she explained. "Perhaps Oswald is destined to communicate with the gods. Leave the bird be." Then, the wife of King Aethelfrith added in a sterner tone before the servant exited the room, "But watch the raven. See that she does no harm to my son."

"Yes, Milady," answered Hazel as she continued to clutch Prince Oswald. Nevertheless, there was still terror in her eyes when she looked at the huge corvid. It mattered not to her that the raven was in communion with the gods. She knew the creature was a scavenger—a flesh-eater. She thought of her younger brother who had recently lost his life fighting the Britons. This bird or others of her kind had likely eaten her brother's flesh and that of their fallen kinsmen.

She made a warding sign, lest the bird decide to peck out Oswald's eyes or her own while they slept, and went back out into the garden.

The fearsome bird did not harm the boy. Instead, Oswald and his pet raven, Mara, spent all day, every day, together. As first, both family and servants thought the bird mimicked the words of others when she spoke in a human-like voice. Soon, it became clear that Mara used her own words when she held council with the young prince. Best of friends, the raven never left Oswald's side.

Their uncanny friendship sent whispers throughout the kingdom: *"There is strange magic between Oswald and his raven," "The raven carries messages from long-dead kings to the prince,"* and *"The raven is the battle goddess herself come to protect our prince."*

The speculation about Oswald and Mara continued despite the best efforts of his parents, King Aethelfrith and Queen Aacha, to squelch them.

Countless servants and town's people learned over the years it was better to steer clear of young Oswald if he misbehaved than to confront him. The price of a pilfered piece of fruit was nothing compared to the scratches from Mara's claws and bites from her beak if a vendor should confront the boy demanding payment. Though such occasions were rare, as Oswald or his attendant almost always compensated shopkeepers and tradesmen.

616 A.D., York, Kingdoms of Bernica and Deira

Whether Oswald was at the market, on horseback, or sparing with friends, the boy's raven always stood guard. The pair were never seen apart. So it was unusual, when one morning as mist shrouded the hills north of the Humber River, rather than go with Oswald to the market, Mara left her friend to accompany his father, King Aethelfrith, and the army of Bernica and Deira into battle.

"Hurry back," said the young prince to his raven.

"I shall soon return," Mara assured him as she took flight.

Oswald leaned against the wall and considered the bird's behavior. Through the constant raids and confrontations between Aethelfrith's army and anyone the king perceived as favoring his wife's brother, Edwin, and his claim to the Deira throne, the raven had remained with Oswald. He wondered what made today's departure different. But he knew Mara saw things through wise eyes, so there must be a reason why she chose to go with his father.

Oswald wasn't the only one contemplating the raven's behavior. Even Aethelfrith, who believed in the Old Gods and their signs, was uneasy when the raven chose to accompany him as the Northumbrians marched toward Chester.

"Why do you think the raven comes with us?" the king asked the warriors nearest him as the black bird flapped above the army.

"The gods are blessing us," replied one of the soldiers.

Aethelfrith smiled. "Perhaps you are right," he responded before nudging his horse into a canter.

Moments later, he learned from his spies that over a thousand monks from Bangor-Is-Coed Monastery had fasted for three days, then climbed a hill near Chester to pray for the success of Aethelfrith's Welsh opponents. This information seemed to confirm the young prince's bird was a champion of the Old Gods. Indeed, the raven looked like a magical blessing flying above the Anglo-Saxons as they swooped down upon their enemy.

It was then, King Aethelfrith decided to eliminate the Christian holy men. "With the approval of the Old Gods, I cannot lose," said the king to the men nearest him.

The nearby Anglo-Saxons shouted their approval.

"Though they are unarmed," Aethelfrith told his soldiers, "these supposed holy men oppose us with their prayers, and thus, encourage our enemy. This behavior cannot be tolerated. They pray to a foreign god for our defeat. Instead, we will silence their voices."

His soldiers cheered their agreement.

Oswald's raven listened, but said nothing.

Rather than engage the waiting Welsh army, King Aethelfrith directed his forces toward the monks. The first part of the Battle of Chester was quick, for it took little time or effort to strike down a thousand praying monks. As the king had hoped, the Welsh were so shocked at seeing the cruel carnage, that soon confusion and dismay led to their defeat.

Under the unwavering gaze of Mara, Aethelfrith claimed victory on the battlefield, then destroyed the monastery at Bangor. The king's ire knew no bounds as he ordered his men to kill all those at the monastery and to let no stone remained stacked upon another.

A few days later, preceded by Oswald's loudly croaking raven, King Aethelfrith triumphantly returned home.

****

"Perhaps the raven *is* truly linked to the gods," the king told his wife over supper. "Our enemies bent before us like grass before the wind."

Queen Aacha, who loved her husband, children, and brother, nodded, then said, "Mayhaps, if the bird has the gods' ears, she can beseech them for peace."

Aethelfrith laughed. "What need do we have for peace if we're victorious in every battle? Let the Welsh, the Britons, the Scots, the Picts, and especially your brother, pray for an end to war. The defeated and the weak need peace, not the men from Bernica and Deira."

Mara stood on the dining table beside Oswald's plate studying the king and queen. After gently prodding her prince's hand, she stepped closer to him. He leaned his head near to her beak. The bird whispered into his ear in a voice softer than an open grave all that she had seen the day of his father's victory.

Oswald didn't question the king about the slaughter-field of monks. Instead, he stroked the raven's back and considered the repercussions of murdering the innocent.

A few days later, King Aethelfrith, again accompanied by Mara, marched toward Bawtry on the River Idle to confront Raedwald, King of East Anglia.

"Victory will be ours again," the king called to his soldiers, "for Oswald's raven soars above us."

The men, though still tired from their fight at Chester, again cheered in response.

But this time, it was Raedwald who proved the better strategist. He refused to allow the exhausted men from north of the Humber River or their king time to prepare for battle. Ignoring decorum, the East Anglican king, with the

10

disposed Edwin of Deira at his side, unceremoniously attacked Aethelfrith and his forces.

Oswald's far-seeing raven shouted no warning of superior numbers, underhanded strategy, or impending defeat to Aethelfrith. She did not lead the king away from battle or swoop down like a winged warrior and pluck out Raedwald's eyes. Instead, she silently observed the defeat and murder of King Aethelfrith on the banks of the River Idle with her blacker-than-night eyes.

At battle's end, when the dead and dying fighters of Bernica and Diera sprawled on the ground at the mercy of the spears and axes of their opponents, Mara soared above them screeching a raven-speak benediction. Then, she flew home to York.

****

"Aethelfrith is dead," cried Mara again and again as she flapped into the courtyard where Oswald practiced fighting with a sword and shield. After circling above the prince three times, she landed on the ground at Oswald's feet and warned, "We must leave."

"Father is dead?" gasped Oswald as he lowered his weapons. His voice quavered when he asked, "You are sure?"

"The king was slain by the River Idle," croaked Mara. "I saw his torn and bloodied body with my own eyes. Now, hurry! You must hurry from this place."

Though only eleven, Oswald knew the dire consequences for any heir of King Aethelfrith if found by Uncle Edwin. Given the chance, Edwin of Deira would be certain to eliminate Oswald and his brothers to secure his unchallenged claim to the throne of Deira. And by the latest victory, the throne of Bernica as well.

"Come," shouted Oswald to his raven as he raced into the keep. "We must tell Mother what has happened."

Upon hearing of her husband's death, Queen Aacha cried for less than a minute. After drying her eyes, she stood and ordered her servants to pack essentials for her children and herself. "We go north, beyond Hadrian's Wall, to the court of the Dalriadan king, Eochaid Buide at Dunadd. He has been a friend in the past, and on my

11

mother's side of the family, he is a relative by marriage. He will protect us from Edwin."

616 A.D., Isle of Mull, Scots Dalriada

Oswald shifted his weight in an attempt to get into a more comfortable position on the horse he was riding. One of King Eochaid Buide's men glanced at him, but said nothing.

The men from Dalriada spoke Gaelic, while he spoke Anglo-Saxon and had only learned a few words of their language, so it was natural that they made no attempt to interact with him. Unfortunately, their silence only emphasized his loneliness. Oswald's mother, younger brother, Oswiu, and his other siblings remained at court. Only Oswald had been sent south to the monks of Iona for education and safekeeping—though his mother promised to send Oswiu to join him when the boy was older.

Suddenly, above his head Mara squawked, "The water. The wide water is before us."

Oswald looked ahead, but only saw more trees, rocks, and grassy hillocks. "I can't see it," he responded.

The raven dropped lower. Still announcing the presence of water, she fluttered in front of the small band of riders as they crested a slight rise and had their first unobstructed view of the Sound of Iona and the small isle where Columba and his Irish monks had landed fifty years earlier.

The leader of their group pointed to a cluster of buildings at the edge of the sea. "Fionnphort," he said. Then, the warrior urged his horse to quicken its pace.

The rest of the Scots Dalriadans and Oswald followed suit. With mounts at a trot, it only took a few minutes for the group to reach the village. Without being told to do so, Oswald slid from his mount and grabbed the sack containing his possessions. Wanting to acknowledge the long journey his escorts had made for a stranger, he did his best to thank them in broken Gaelic. The men smiled, then answered him. Their leader even made an attempt to say farewell in Anglo-Saxon before heading back to King Eochaid Buide's court.

Mara perched on a nearby pile of fishing nets muttering to herself as the Fionnphort ferryman helped Oswald into a boat for the final leg of his journey.

"Do you want to ride in the boat?" Oswald called to Mara as the ferryman pushed off from shore.

If the raven responded, the wind stole her words, for Oswald heard nothing from his friend as she leapt into the wind.

Luckily, Oswald didn't get sick as the small craft bobbed in the white-capped waves of the sound. Perhaps, it was because he was too busy studying the rocky island which was to be his new home. More likely, it was because he was watching Mara play tag with a flock of gulls flying alongside the boat.

She would shout, "Away, away," at the noisy birds before diving down toward the boat and chasing them off. Next, the raven would soar higher and the gulls would return. Whereupon, Mara would dive down and scare the gulls again. The game persisted until the boat reached port on Iona.

Once he had disembarked from the watercraft, Oswald tried to thank the ferryman, who much like King Eochaid Buide's men, smiled and waved in response.

Uncertain what to do next, he began to walk from the dock toward a cluster of buildings which he thought might be the monastery. Mara sailed above him, but offered no comment on his current situation.

"Oswald?" asked a short man as he approached him.

Despite the chilly wind, Oswald noticed the man wore no heavy cloak, only sandals and a coarse woolen garment over a lighter-colored tunic.

"Yes," he answered. "And my raven, Mara."

Upon hearing her name, his raven landed on the street beside Oswald and bowed her head to the monk.

"No one said anything about a raven," responded the man. "But I suppose if a raven was kind enough to feed Elijah in the *Book of Kings*, then one will be good company for the brothers on Iona."

"Good company," cawed Mara as she once more lifted into the air.

13

"She is a clever one," observed the monk. "I imagine you are, too." He tapped his chest, "I am Brother Liam, and you must be Oswald."

"Yes." Oswald paused, even though the words were thickly accented, the monk had spoken to him in Anglo-Saxon. "You know my language!"

Brother Liam nodded. "I know enough to help you learn Gaelic—which is only one of the subjects you will be taught during your stay with us. Now, come. Let us walk to the monastery."

623 A.D., Isle of Iona, Scots Dalriada

Oswald and Mara rested upon a rock on the hill above *Dun Bhuirg*, an ancient fort on the west side of Iona. From their position, they could view not only dozens of tiny islands dotting the water near Iona, but *Camus Cul an Taibh*—the Bay at the Back of the Ocean. Oswald felt he knew every nook and cranny, bird, wildflower, island, and named hillock which made up his adopted home. Just like he knew each of the monks who lived at the monastery in their beehive huts.

It was hard for him to believe he had resided among the brothers for seven years. They'd taught him to read and write in Latin as well as Gaelic. Even Mara could speak Gaelic nearly as well as Anglo-Saxon.

As he thought of his raven, he reached out and caressed her shimmery back. "We will be leaving soon, I expect."

"Soon," agreed Mara.

"But the monks have my brother Oswiu to educate now. They won't miss us too much."

"Miss us," replied the raven with a nod of her softly feathered head. "Miss us more than you know."

Oswald stood, then brushed off the back of his cloak. He had grown taller and more muscular over the years with the brothers. So much so, that his left shoulder was now large and strong enough to serve as Mara's perch when they traveled together.

As if reading his thoughts, the raven flapped to his shoulder. Croaking occasionally, she hung on tightly with her claws as Oswald made his way across the meadows to a small peak due west of the monastery's border wall. The brothers had nicknamed the location, *Sgurr an Fhithich*— The Raven's Peak, since Mara often perched among the few windswept ash trees which grew there when she watched the brothers tend their cattle and sheep.

"Even on Saturday, they work," observed Oswald as several of the monks gathered vegetables from the garden below them.

"They work and work," said Mara as she ruffled her feathers. "It is their life."

"We have worked beside them in the gardens, too. Helped them build new wickerwork huts, stone cells, and a larger oratory. Welcomed hundreds of pilgrims to Columba's grave. It has been a good life."

"A good life," said his raven.

Oswald smiled remembering Mara's efforts in the garden. The raven liked to work alongside the monks. Using her sharp eyes and quicker than a dagger beak, she spotted, grabbed, then consumed all of the insect pests within her reach. She'd even tried to help gather the turf for the huts and cheerfully welcomed newcomers. Though many of their visitors were taken aback by a talking raven. Some had even considered her an ill omen.

"Our boat," said Mara as she nudged Oswald's chin to look southeast.

He turned his head in the direction of the port and saw a watercraft approaching the dock. He suspected Mara was correct. King Eochaid Buide had promised to send for him when he was old enough to serve in the court as a translator and bodyguard. He owed the Scots Dalriadan ruler for not only saving his life, but that of his mother and siblings. It was time to pay back the debt.

623 A.D., Dunadd, Scots Dalriada

King Eochaid Buide's court at Dunadd was much as Oswald remembered it from his brief time there with his mother before he had been sent to Iona. And the king himself had changed little, though the his famous yellow locks were now streaked with gray. Granted, the Scots Dalriadans and their king were welcoming, but he

15

suspected Dunadd would have been an even friendlier place had his sister, Aebbe, agreed to marry Prince Domnall Brecc mac Eochaid three years earlier rather than enter a nunnery. But that was her choice, and now, nothing but water under the bridge.

A quick scan of the town through the eyes of an adult, rather than those of a frightened eleven-year-old boy, revealed Dunadd's location perched on a rocky, high hillside surrounded by *Moine Mhor,* the Great Moss, made it an extremely defensible fortress. It didn't take long for Oswald to see that the town was overflowing with warriors eager to prove their worth. Now that he was fluent in Gaelic, Oswald easily struck up friendships with many in the royal family including the king's son, Domnall, and his cousin visiting from the northern vales of Ireland, Connad Cerr mac Conall.

"Oswald, you should have been with us last year at the Battle of Cenn Delgthan," said Domnall. "We sent Ui Neill and his allies running."

"Sent them running," said Mara in Gaelic.

The prince clapped his hands. "Ho! It seems your raven can translate into Anglo-Saxon if you are not about."

Oswald smiled, then nodded. "But you could never be certain she would do what you asked her to do. Mara has a mind of her own sometimes." He reached up to his left shoulder and scratched the raven on the side of her neck.

"Mind of my own," agreed Mara with a tilt of her head.

"And sometimes, Mara keeps information to herself," added Oswald.

"Nevertheless, flying above and before us, she would be an asset in battle," said Connad Cerr thoughtfully. "She could discover and report on the enemy's positions with little danger to herself."

"Wouldn't your opponents spot her and suspect something was amiss? Perhaps even shoot her from the sky?" asked Oswald.

"No," responded Connad Cerr. "Many Irish believe in The Morrigan, three battle goddesses who take the form of ravens. To shoot at Mara would be like trying to kill a merciless goddess who decides your fate in battle."

16

"Cousin, if we cross the channel again to Ireland, we will invite Oswald and his raven," promised Domnall. "But enough talk of war," he continued, "it is time for evening meal. Let us proceed to the dining hall."

"To the dining hall," agreed Mara with a click of her beak.

"Indeed," said Oswald, "for even a war goddess must eat."

628 A.D., Dunadd, Scots Dalriada

"I cannot believe King Eochaid Buide is dead," Oswald said as he stroked Mara's back. "He is the reason my family and I are still alive."

Mara turned her head and rubbed against his hand.

"Connad Cerr mac Conall is now King of Dalriada. He remembers my words of five years ago, and wants us to travel with him to Ireland to fight Mael Caich and the Irish Cruithne." Oswald looked out over the green lowlands that encircled Dunadd. "Even though I would rather stay here, we must go."

The raven studied his face for a moment, then said, "We must go."

629 A.D., Northern Ireland

The night before they landed in Ireland, Oswald had a dream. In his dream, King Connad Cerr and many other brave Scots Dalriadans from Dunadd laid dead on the battlefield. He only told his dream to Mara, for he knew to warn the king or any of his warriors would be useless. King Connad was determined to answer the battle call from his allies across the channel.

Mara listened, then touched his cheek with her beak. "You will not die in Ireland," she said.

"Maybe or maybe not." Oswald hadn't even considered if he could be one of the bodies he had seen. "In battle, we all take our chances."

"You will return alive and well to Dunadd," the raven assured him. "I have seen it."

17

"You cannot know that," responded Oswald. An image of his mother grieving flashed in his mind.

"I *know* you will return to Dunadd," said Mara. "For it is not yet your time."

****

The fighting at the Battle of Fid Eoin was fierce. The beating of sword against shield, the clang of metal meeting metal, and the screams of the wounded filled the Irish air along with the stink of blood and death.

Mara flew above Oswald crying, "Away! Stay back!"

When a warrior chose to engage Oswald, the raven dove at him flapping her wings, scratching with her claws, and screeching, "Death! Death!" But she always managed to dart out of the way before Oswald brought his sword down on his opponent.

Many in the enemy faction of Irishmen hesitated to engage the tall blond man with the guardian raven. Oswald heard them calling, "Beware, he's a favorite of The Morrigan. Watch out for the raven. There are plenty of other Scots to kill."

Whether it was luck, destiny, or superstition on the part of the Irish, Oswald retreated unharmed to the Irish shore with the rest of the defeated Scots Dalriadans. It offered little comfort to him that they were able to carry the body of King Connad to a boat and sail him back home, because they were forced to leave the rest of their dead, many of them dear friends, as a feast for ravens and other scavengers.

Though he did not say anything to Mara about the flocks of ravens descending onto the battlefield and tearing the bodies of the dead Scots warriors, some of the Dalriadans gave his friend angry glances.

"I do not consume the dead," she loudly proclaimed from his shoulder, "just as all men do not slaughter monks."

Oswald saw puzzled looks on the faces of the Scotsmen. They didn't know to what the raven referred, but he recalled Mara's description of what his father, King Aethelfrith, had done at the Battle of Chester thirteen years prior.

"No, Mara, you are different from many of your kind," he said as he climbed into the boat and they set sail for Dunadd.

18

629 A.D. Dunadd, Scots Dalriada

Oswald's old friend and King Eochaid Buide's son, Domnall Brecc mac Eochaid, was crowned King of the Scots Dalmatians upon their return to Dunadd. Though he was happy to be back on familiar soil, Oswald longed for the quiet days of study, prayer, and farming among the monks at Iona.

The overwhelming desire to return to the monastery and its daily routine reaffirmed what Oswald knew: even though his father, King Aethelfrith, had been a die-hard believer in the Old Gods, he was a Christian. Comforted by being a Christian among other Christians in Dalriada, nevertheless he found he longed to bring his adopted faith to the people of Northumbria. But his uncle, King Edwin, still ruled Bernica and Deira.

When he shared his desire to bring the new religion to his birthplace, Mara rubbed her beak against his cheek. "Patience," said the raven. "Things happen in their own time."

633 A.D., Dunadd, Scots Dalriada

A great hooray echoed throughout Dunadd when news reached the town of King Edwin's death on October twelfth at the Battle of Hatfield Chase. But the joy of Oswald and the Scots Dalriadans was short-lived. The victors, Penda of Mercia and the Welsh King Cadwallon ap Cadfan of Gwynedd, immediately began to slaughter as many Northumbrians as they could find.

"I need to return home and help my people," Oswald told Mara as they sat by the fire late at night after everyone else had gone to their bedchambers.

"Not yet," croaked the raven. "Not yet, Oswald."
****
Next, word came from Bernica that Oswald's half-brother, Eanfrith, had returned from exile in Pictland to assume kingship of the northern portion of Northumbria. At the same time, Osric, a cousin of Oswald's mother,

returned to Deira to become king of the southern part of Northumbria. But still, Cadwallon of Gwynedd persisted.

First, Cadwallon slayed Osric. The men of Deira who survived the fight, scattered in fear. Next, Eanfrith, under a flag of truce with only twelve Bernican guardsmen, went to negotiate a peace with the Welsh. King Cadwallon lured in the trusting Eanfrith, then had Oswald's half-brother and his men murdered.

Angered by the evil of his brother's and cousin's betrayals, Oswald told Mara, "We cannot sit by any longer and do nothing. Now, we *must* return to Northumbria and fight."

"Now, we must fight," agreed the raven.

****

"The time has come for me to go home and save my people," said Oswald to King Domnall Brecc mac Eochaid of Dalriada.

"Save the people," croaked Mara from her perch on Oswald's shoulder.

King Domnall nodded. "I will support your cause," he assured his friend. "And I will send word to Iona. Some of the monks will want to fight for you, too."

Oswald gripped Domnall's right arm with both hands. "Thank you and the Scots Dalriadans for all you have done for me and my family. We will be in your debt forever."

"Forever," said Mara, first in Gaelic, then in Anglo-Saxon.

"I think even the raven knows you are headed south to your homeland," said King Domnall.

"She always knows more than she tells," replied Oswald with a grim smile on his face.

"More than I tell," croaked the raven.

634 A.D., Hexham, Northumbria

Oswald, with Mara perched on his shoulder, stood on a rise and looked over the landscape. Positioning his men between Brady's Crag and Hadrian's Wall was as good a defensive position as any. And Oswald's forces, which included men of Northumbria from Bernica and Deira, the Scots Dalriadans, and the monks of Iona, would need a

20

good defensive position to compensate for the much larger Welsh force which approached them.

Oswald knew that the Welsh king, Cadwallon, murderer of his half-brother, Eanfrith, and cousin, Osric, along with countless numbers of Oswald's countrymen, women, and children, would show no mercy if tomorrow's battle didn't go the Northumbrians' way.

"I am afraid for Northumbria, Dalriada, even Iona," Oswald whispered to Mara.

The raven rubbed her beak against his cheek. "You will not fall. You will not fail," the bird assured her friend. "Victory will be tomorrow's outcome."

"I hope you're right. But still, I worry." With a sigh, Oswald sat down, leaned against the trunk of a tree, and closed his eyes.

He awoke with a start about a half an hour later. He'd had another dream: He was back on Iona, kneeling by Saint Columba's grave. Columba came to him, and told him to build a large wooden cross on the field where the battle would play out.

"Come," he called to a nearby group of Scots Dalriadans and Iona monks. "We must construct a wooden cross before the battle." When he saw the puzzled looks of his friends, he added, "Saint Columba came to me in a dream and told me this must be done if we're to be victorious."

Without questioning their leader further, the monks and Dalriadans felled two trees. Using battle axes, swords, and knives, they shaped a towering wooden cross. Trusting both Oswald and their faith, the men helped raise the cross by moonlight on the night prior to the battle outside Hexham. Then, beside Oswald, they knelt and prayed to the Christian God for victory.

When the men bowed their heads in prayer, Mara left Oswald's shoulder. She flew around the cross three times, then alighted on one of its arms. "Victory," she said before returning to stand on the grass by her old friends, the monks from Iona.

****

The Welsh, led by King Cadwallon, attacked in the morning. The location selected by Oswald forced the Welsh to approach the Northumbrians and their allies along a narrow front. So narrow that their superior numbers meant little.

As Oswald led his men to meet Welsh, the sounds and sights of the long ago battle in Ireland were repeated. But this time, it was his enemies who were routed. The retreat soon became a disorganized flight. As the army of Cadwallon ap Cadfan of Gwynedd ran, Oswald caught up with the Welsh king at the Brook of Denis and killed him.

When Oswald and his army returned to the initial location of the fighting, the monks surrounded the cross, knelt down, and proclaimed the altercation would evermore be known as The Battle of Heavenfield. The Northumbrians, most still followers of the Old Gods, had witnessed the power of Oswald's God, and many joined the monks and Dalriadans in embracing Christianity. But not all.

Mara held tight to Oswald's shoulder as the men celebrated their victory, new king, and new religion. She kept silent during their hurrahs, hail-to-the-kings, and prayers to both the Old Gods and the Christian God.

"Now," whispered Oswald to his raven, "perhaps Bernica and Deira can prosper in peace as a strong, united Northumbria."

"Perhaps," said Mara.

Though he did not press the raven for more information, Oswald was somewhat unsettled by Mara's lukewarm endorsement of his hopes for long lasting peace, prosperity, and unity in Northumbria.

635 A.D. Royal Court at Bamburgh, Northumbria

"You have come," exclaimed King Oswald as he clasped the hand of Bishop Aidan, a monk trained in the ways of Iona.

"I am happy to serve the Kingdom of Northumbria and her king," answered Aidan in Gaelic.

"I am giving the island of Lindisfarne to the Church for use as a monastery," explained Oswald. "The Christianity of Iona and of your own Scattery Island are the faith I want for my people."

"I am honored to spread Irish Christianity to Northumbria, but I will need a translator. I do not speak the language of the Anglo-Saxons," said Aidan.

"I humbly offer my services." King Oswald pressed the palm of his right hand to his chest. "That is, when my duties here allow me the time."

"Offer my services, too," said Mara in Gaelic.

Bishop Aidan raised his eyebrows, then spoke, "This must be the raven I have heard much about."

King Oswald rubbed Mara's neck with his forefinger. "This is Mara, my companion since childhood. She speaks both Gaelic and Anglo-Saxon, but I do not think she is the wisest choice for a translator—her penmanship is terrible."

Oswald and Bishop Aidan both laughed.

****

Months later, while accompanying Bishop Aidan to Lindisfarne, a group of poor women and children approached King Oswald begging alms.

"What food have we with us?" Oswald asked his guards.

The soldiers pulled back the covering from a small wagon loaded with vittles.

Oswald dismounted, went to the wagon, and under the watchful eyes of his raven and the bishop, gave away most of the food to the beggars gathered around him. Then, he opened a cloth-wrapped bundle, removed his personal silverware, broke it apart, and handed the pieces of precious metal to the children.

Bishop Aidan, dismounted, walked to Oswald, grasped his right hand, and said, "May this hand never perish."

"Never perish," Mara said as she studied the bishop.

August 642 A.D., Maserfelth, Britain

In the twilight quiet, King Oswald sat on a fallen tree's trunk looking out over the Maserfelth countryside. Mara perched beside him. Not far away, as always these past few years, a dozen guards watched and listened.

"They call me *Bretwalda* now," mused Oswald, "King of all Saxon England. The title seems both a blessing and a curse."

"Both," said Mara as she turned to face her friend.

"But at least I didn't have to fight for it all." Oswald rubbed his chin, pulled lightly at his short, blond beard. "While Oswiu and I had to conquer Nodding, Wessex came to me with my marriage to King Cynegils's daughter, and North Rheged joined our kingdom when Oswiu married Princess Rhianinfelt. Those were peaceful take-overs."

"Peaceful take-overs," echoed the raven.

"And I've never forgotten my allies. I always send men when King Domnall Brecc of Scots Dalriada asks. Though I wish he would give up on acquiring more land from the Picts and Irish. Mara," he said as he stroked her back, "I think I've seen enough war. Tomorrow, will be my last battle."

"Your last battle," agreed Mara before edging even closer to the King of all Saxon England as Oswald gazed at the first stars appearing in the dimming sky.

****

The skies on the morning of August fifth were even bluer than Oswald's eyes when King Penda of Mercia led not only his army, but the united Welsh armies of Gwynedd, Powys, and Pengwern against the Anglo-Saxons. Though Oswald and his men fought ferociously, it was not enough.

When it became apparent his death was close at hand, Oswald shouted to his raven, "Leave me, Mara. Fly to safety."

"I will fly to safety, but I shall never leave you," replied Mara as she winged her way to a nearby ash tree.

From her elevated position, the raven watched the Mercians and Welsh swarm over the battlefield like ants. She gazed down at her friend at the end when Oswald prayed for his men as they fell around him. When at last his enemies reached the King of all Saxon England, Mara observed them hack his body into dozens of pieces. Then, in celebration of the defeat of the Christian king, the Mercians and Welsh, who still worshiped the Old Gods, stuck Oswald's head and both arms on poles and left them for the scavengers. Though the enemy didn't notice her, this vile behavior was observed by the unblinking eyes of the Oswald's raven.

When the Mercian and Welsh warriors began to depart the Maserfelth battlefield, Mara swooped from her perch, grabbed Oswald's right arm, then returned to the ash tree. For days, high up in the ash tree, the raven held the arm blessed by Bishop Aidan years earlier. Finally, she could hold onto it no longer. But it was reported by men of the Saxon army and local people alike that where Oswald's arm finally fell, a holy spring burst forth from the earth—a spring with healing powers.

The ravens, who usually ate the bodies of the battle dead, were said to refuse to touch the head, arms, and the rest of King Oswald. Instead, men from Northumbria buried Oswald's remains, save his head and arms, on the battlefield where he fell while legions of ravens, led by Mara, spiraled overhead calling, "Oswald. Oswald."

The arms were transported back to the Northumbrian Royal Seat of Bamburgh where they were enshrined in silver and kept in the Church of St. Oswald. His head was taken to Lindisfarne and buried at the Cathedral at Durham. Soldiers, monks, and everyday citizens alike witnessed Oswald's raven faithfully staying with the king's head as it was transported to Lindisfarne monastery.

Even after Oswald's head was safely buried at Lindisfarne, the raven would not leave. The monks fed Mara, and occasionally conversed with her in both Anglo-Saxon and Gaelic. She was known to even quote scripture in Latin to the brothers who visited with her. It was reported in over three decades-worth of notes written by the Lindisfarne monks that the raven never left Oswald's head for more than a few minutes each day when she would fly outside and circle the monastery three times crying, "Oswald. Oswald. I shall never leave you."

On August fifth, exactly thirty-two years after King Oswald of all Saxon England had died, the monk who entered the room where Oswald's head was kept, found Mara—dead. The raven lay on her side atop the small casket which held the King of all Saxon England's head. Though not officially condoned by the bishop, quietly the faithful raven's body was slipped inside the wooden box with Saint Oswald's perfectly-preserved head.

When Bishop Cuthbert of Lindisfarne died in March 687 A.D., the monks re-buried Saint Oswald's head in Cuthbert's casket. Thereafter, in illuminated manuscripts and other religious art, Saint Cuthbert was often shown holding a second head. But what was not shown, though the monks of Lindisfarne knew it should be, was that in addition to Saint Oswald's head, hidden in Cuthbert's casket was the miraculously-preserved body of a raven.

For none of the monks had the heart to separate Mara, Oswald's raven, from her friend.

720 A.D., The Abbey Church of Saint Peter and Saint Paul, Monkweamouth-Jarrow, Northumbria

Brother Bede sat at his table and studied his notes about Oswald of Northumbria and his raven, Mara. At first, tales of the uncommon friendship between the bird and the saintly Oswald seemed unlikely. But Bede was thorough in his investigation: gathering firsthand and secondhand accounts, visiting known locations, studying notes written by the monks at Iona and Lindisfarne on the edges of manuscripts, copying letters and other correspondences between the players in this drama, and praying for guidance on the question of Oswald's raven.

He wanted his *Historia Ecclesiastica Gentis Anglorum* [*Ecclesiastical History of the English People*] to be accurate. Two books nearly completed, he was hard at work on the third volume. The only question: Were tales of Oswald's raven legend or truth?

Again, he looked at the map of Iona and tapped his forefinger on a rise labeled *The Raven's Peak*. Second, he flipped to an old map of England. There by the Welsh border was Oswestry or "Oswald's Tree," not far from the Maserfelth battlefield. And drawn in black ink by the village was a tree and a raven.

Next, he studied two illuminated manuscripts which told of King Oswald, a saint by both martyrdom and miracles. On both, the illustration of Saint Oswald showed him with not only a crown, scepter, orb, sword, and ciborium, but with a raven. He placed his hand on the nearest stack of evidence and frowned. No matter *his* conclusions, he suspected the ship had already set sail on the raven legend.

Lastly, he unwrapped a black feather from inside a rolled piece of parchment. Upon the parchment, the bishop of Lindisfarne had written:

Dear Venerable Bede,

As to your questions about Oswald's raven, I can only relay what I have been told, since the bird died on 5 August 674 A.D.

According to several older monks who still reside at Lindisfarne, the bird was able to converse in Gaelic and Anglo-Saxon, as well as Latin. These skills seem to have been learned at the monastery on Iona.

The brothers tell me that the raven stayed with Saint Oswald's head from its arrival at Lindisfarne until the bird's death. It was then decided, without approval of Church leaders, to place the raven's body in the casket with Oswald's head.

Upon the arrival of Saint Cuthbert's body in 687, the decision was made to place Saint Oswald's head into the same casket as Cuthbert. The monks have explained to me, that at that time (again without approval of the monastery's leadership) the raven was also place in Cuthbert's casket beside Oswald's head.

Another interesting fact I gleaned from these monks is that when transferred to Saint Cuthbert's casket. not only was Saint Oswald's head in perfect condition—surely preserved by his saintly nature and the goodness of God— but that the body of the raven was also unnaturally well- preserved. I can only explain the bird's incorruptible condition—even in death—to be the result of her association with a saint.

Your fellow servant in the Lord's Church,

The Bishop of Lindisfarne

Bede placed the bishop's letter with the rest of the evidence. Then, while he twirled the black feather between his fingertips, he decided to err on the side of caution and include Oswald's raven in the history books.

Morrigan and Odin's Ravens

Colleen Anderson

Two gods led northern races
obsessed with bloodshed passions
that ran as high as tides
pure as sea-spanning winds
unquenchable as volcanic fire

The gods could not resist competition
over ravens as if there were too few
to go around the arena of their desires
wings feverishly fanning lusts
so they forged the middle realm

Morrigan charged her ravens
to scour battlefields, lift up
the souls of the dying and the dead
convey them home to roost

Odin ordered two to snoop
gouge Midgard's belly
scoop secrets from men and women
the corvid couple divvied up the lot

Morrigan needed three to dive
into the pathways of past
present and yet to be seen
to carry off spirits from the land
of living to introspective realms
life suspended and spaces in between

Odin left the ken of mortal men
up to his godling children
scribed the sky with winged couriers
seeking more scholarly pursuits

devouring all with his singular sight
divided between mind and matter

On days gravid with dark clouds
somber thoughts, and grief thick enough to stir
Morrigan's ravens convey those slain
while Odin's sort thoughts and memories
of shades whose mortal coils twist away
their ephemera kept for taste and touch
when glory of the gods has faded

The title comes from the connection of the ash tree to the element of fire, as well as being a reference to Norse mythology of the World Tree. With the name Yggdrasil, this was a giant ash tree at the center of the universe connecting the various worlds and with roots extending to under regions and branches reaching above and to the sides of the human world. The human world is at the center and therefore one of the main things "under" the ash. This works well as a metaphor to pull together the various material included in this collection since it considers more than one simple world. You won't be bored with just one subject or form of poetry.

https://www.hiraethsffh.com/product-page/under-the-ash-by-shelly-bryant

The Butcher's Dog
Peri Dwyer Worrell

Hector sold me, but I'm sure it was a mistake.

I sat erect under the corrugated metal shelter over the Mercado Veinteocho de Febrero in Cuenca, Ecuador. The other dogs dropped their tails, curled their ears, and slunk around me, and quite rightly. I barely even acknowledged them (unless there was a bitch in heat, of course). Why should I? My sleek fur and soft contours clearly demonstrated my superiority in contrast to their dull coats, their gaunt ribs.

It was all due to my loyal and loving natural devotion to Hector the butcher. The booth I guarded at night was full of delectable whole chickens, sides of pigs hung on hooks above the pigs' heads on the counter, and scrumptious donuts of ground beef. I lapped blood from the concrete before it could disappear down the drain in the center of the floor. I nibbled scraps of skin and fat that flew when the cleaver came down on flesh positioned on the gouged and stained wood block.

The customers came day in and day out: stocky, serious *indigenas* buying chickens complete with feet and head in a separate package; restaurateurs who'd buy an entire half pig and minutely oversee the cuts; every now and then a rich *gringa* who'd demand the fat be trimmed away, the feet and heads discarded. The last were my favorite, because I got the scraps.

Hector took their money and gave them their meat. One day, instead of meat, he took a man's money and instead of meat, he gave them me.

Perhaps I should explain my background. First, know that I'm of a herding breed. Think of a border collie, or an Australian shepherd. Then think of generations of my ancestors weaving our way through the untidy traffic of Andean towns cities. The dullards among us don't survive to breed. I don't mean to brag, here. It's just a simple

30

statement of fact that we're among the smartest dogs in the world.

My mother was in charge of herding an entire rural flock, mixed goats and alpacas, and it was poetry in motion to watch her agility as she guided them along the steepest ravines or expertly cut the very one the owner designated out of the flock. One morning well before dawn, when I was not yet a year old, I pranced along at the heels of the herder's son one morning when he went to bargain with the meat distributor.

The meat distributor, Raul, eyed me with admiration. His gaze kept falling on me during the preliminary small talk with the youth. I followed the transactions easily, watching hands and faces, nods and body language, smelling the puffs of social pheromones as they wavered. When their business was done, it was obvious to me that I'd been part of the transaction. I licked the boy's hand, once only, and lay down at the meat distributor's feet.

Around sunrise, after another session of bargaining, I trotted out of the warehouse a few inches behind the left heel of the butcher—Hector. I'd been thrown into a bargain that Raul had pressed hard to make. No need to be indignant: this happens to pups, at least the lucky ones who aren't driven out into the streets or thrown off cliffs in burlap bags. This is a poor country and pets are a luxury.

I followed him to the loading dock, where I sat silently, ears forward. I was assessing Hector, and watching him supervise the carcasses loaded on his truck, I decided he was forthright, calm, and fair. He struck me an alpha with nothing to prove. His body odor bespoke moderation but not abstention.

I approved of the man; I was content with my fate.

When loading finished, at a nod from Hector, I jumped into the truck's cab and took my place on the passenger-side floorboard.

That first glorious day at the mercado, I could hardly believe my luck! At dusk, we returned to Hector's home, a walled compound of wooden buildings on stilts, set into a hillside. His children ran up squealing to meet the new dog. After ear-scratching and hand-licking, I investigated a hutch of cuys, little edible rodents that they kept for holiday

31

meat. Hector's wife eyed me warily as I sniffed the free-ranging chickens until she was satisfied that I wouldn't kill one. When it got cold that night, I found a warm spot next to the kitchen wall where the fire was banked in the corner and curled up for the night.

I was home.

*   *   *

But when this event of which I speak happened, I was five years old, already in love with Hector, proud of my place at his feet, reveling in the carnivorous feast before me every day, basking in the sunshine in the thin mountain air. I felt sure I was set for life.

Then the gringo Charlie walked into the mercado. I knew him as a regular customer, smelling, as usual, like too much mint and not enough garlic, combined with a chemical disinfectant smell I intensely disliked. Today he also smelled just recovered from a cold, overlaid with the lovely funky sweat of recent sex. Visually, he looked soft and pale, as always, and he laughed his normal harshly nervous laugh that set my neck hairs twitching. However, I ignored the laugh and wagged my tail, drooling, because he usually pinched off a tiny piece of ground meat and flicked it to me right after Hector weighed it. He picked out his meats for the week and spoke intently with Hector. I gave a tiny yip of surprise when I realized by their looks at me and their body language, the smells of Hector's reluctance and greed and the gringo's determination and triumph, that I was part of today's deal.

When it was done, Charlie clicked his tongue.

"Mashi," he called me. I followed, stiff-legged, looking repeatedly back at Hector, expecting him to correct the mistake, but he ignored me. The smell if his regret was the only goodbye I got.

To add insult to injury, when I walked past the seamstress's booth down the aisle, my distress emboldened her creepy little dachshund. He darted out and nipped at my hind leg, an effrontery he'd never have assayed the day before. I was forced to pin him down with a snarl. His yips and growls attracted everyone's attention. The seamstress whipped a scrap of velvet at her dog and he scrambled back.

32

Charlie grabbed my scruff and spoke sternly to me in English. He slipped a collar around my neck and clipped a leash to it, the first time I'd ever been bound. I was stunned as I followed him. This did not bode well for my future.

Charlie took me to his home, a suite of rooms facing the courtyard on the second floor of a thick-walled colonial building. I lived indoors, an odd sensation. We went out every day for a walk in the neighborhood. I didn't understand the words of his commands at first, since he spoke to me in English, but his meaning was usually clear. It took me a day or two to figure out that he said, "sit," for "*siéntete*," for example.

He'd walk with me each morning to the city park, cautioning me to "Stay... Stay.... Stay," every few seconds, until finally "Go!" I would spring forward and race up and down the grassy meadows with abandon. Charlie would ignore me. I would pause on a small rise at the end of the park closest to the mercado, sniffing the air for the smells of the goods sold there, but especially for the meat smell. When I caught that iron-blood aroma, I examined it for the slightest trace of Hector's familiar odor.

I found out that the chemical smell I'd noticed the first day was concentrated, in a room at the end of his suite. He entered it only after donning booties, plastic gloves, a coverall, and a plastic face shield. I was not invited to follow. When Charlie went in there, I lay across the doorway and waited, sometimes for hours. The solitude and boredom of those hours weighed on me. I was trying to be a good dog for Charlie, but I missed Hector. My relationship with Charlie was missing a certain intimacy.

* * *

One day, we came home from our early-morning walk and Charlie disappeared into the room. He came out after a short time holding a syringe.

"Here you go, boy!" he said. I wagged my tail, since that was his phrase when he tossed me a scrap, but instead he knelt, pinched up the skin on my neck, and injected me with the contents of the syringe. "You're officially CRISPRed!" He gave his jerky laugh.

33

I felt odd immediately. My heart beat faster and I felt like I might vomit. I stumbled to my stuffed bed in the corner and lay down.

I slept the rest of the day; it was twilight when I awakened. My throat was sore and my nose was dry. I shook my head and immediately regretted it, as the room spun. I reeled to my water bowl and lapped up so much water that I did vomit a little, which hurt my sore throat terribly.

I was not a well dog. Charlie stood over me, writing in a notebook. I collapsed on my belly then, and after a few minutes he scooped me up and carried me back to my bed.

I stayed in that bed for a few days, turning up my nose at the meals Charlie put in front of me, often putting my paws over my eyes to block the painful daylight, my ears folded to block the normal city sounds, now acutely amplified. A couple of times, Charlie disturbed me to draw blood from my foreleg, but that barely registered through the fog of pain and nausea.

But eventually I began to feel better. One morning, I still had a dull headache, but now I was ravenously hungry. I walked over to my untouched meal from the day before, chicken offal, *mote*, and broth, and began to eat.

What a strange sensation as I worked my tongue and teeth! As a dog, I had no lips to speak of, but my mouth muscles quivered oddly around my jowls and chin. When I swallowed, something in my throat quivered, a new sensation I'd never felt before.

Charlie noticed I was up.

"You're eating, Mashi! Good boy!" I beat my tail on the floor. "Is that good, Mashi? Is it good?"

As naturally as my tail wagged, I raised my head and made a noise. It wasn't exactly a bark.

"Goooo," I said.

Charlie's eyebrows shot up. His smell signaled excitement. He grabbed his notebook and scribbled something.

"Mashi." My tail thumped again. "Is that…*goooooood*?" he drew out the sounds carefully and my eyes were drawn to his mouth.

34

My mouth and throat seemed out of my control as I formed the syllable back at him, "Gooooo." I couldn't make the "d" sound so I ended the word with a little shrill yip.

"Yes!" Charlie made a fist and did a little dance. My tail thumped a few more times. Suddenly I was exhausted again. I walked to my bed and collapsed, leaving Charlie to scribble.

*   *   *

As I regained my health, we continued our routine of daily walks and I gradually built my endurance back up in the park. I never stopped pausing on the rise, and now I could form the sounds of the word, "Hector" as I sniffed the breeze coming from the mercado.

I regained the weight I'd lost, though my coat was never as lush as it had been when I was the butcher's dog, king of the mercado.

Charlie was irritable. Mainly it seemed, he was angry that he couldn't tell anyone about me.

"Mashi," tail thump, "they wouldn't understand, would they, boy?" He'd scratch my ears. "But you won't die on me, will you? Might even outlive me, won't you? And you're a *real* best friend, aren't you a real best friend?"

"Veshk ren(yip)," I'd answer. *Best friend.* Each time I tried to make a phoneme my mouth was unsuited for, I got a little closer. But a full nasal stop while voicing was still tricky for me. And my changing face refused to grow lips.

Now, dogs don't lie. That's part of why people love dogs, I think. But a really smart dog, such as, for example, a herding breed that's been naturally selected for cunning over generations, can mislead, withhold information, or redirect.

I quickly realized that Charlie thought I understood no more language than I could speak. But the truth was, whatever was changing in my body and allowing me to slowly approach intelligible speech, my brain was outpacing it exponentially.

"We'll just have to repeat the blood test a little earlier this week, won't we," Charlie would muse. A lonely man, he spoke to me a lot. I let him think it was in the nature of talking to himself, but inside my head I was thinking, *you'll probably do it Tuesday instead of Thursday because you're*

35

seeing Elena on Thursday this week, aren't you? And Wednesday is your cards night?

"We'll do it Tuesday. Yes we will. Who's my good boy?" Tail thump. "Is it Mashi? Is Mashi a good, good boy?"

"Goo(yip) oy." *Good boy.* I walked up to him for an ear rub, but he was already engrossed in his computer. I missed Hector.

*   *   *

Then came the day Charlie drew blood from my foreleg, then followed it up with an injection that made me immediately fall asleep.

I woke up inside a small box with grating on its windows. The latch was a simple mechanism. Charlie knew by now that I was smart and determined enough to undo most latches, limited only by my lack of thumbs, so he'd added a small combination lock to thwart my efforts.

The box was inside a vehicle, an SUV, and Charlie sat up front, next to the driver. I lay quietly and watched the sky on one side and cliff faces on the other as we wended our way down switchbacks. A few times I spotted alpacas and thought nostalgically of my mother. Finally, after descending many thousands of feet in altitude, the road straightened out onto Ecuador's coastal plateau.

In another hour or two, we stopped at a busy location, which I now know was an airport. At the time, the smell of aviation fuel, thousands of people from all over, the ocean breeze, and the glorious stink of the city of Guayaquil were overwhelmingly strange and new. I stood inside the crate, expecting them to let me out to explore, but instead a stranger loaded the crate on a cart and wheeled me out, to sit in the unfamiliar equatorial heat for hours.

I was eventually loaded into the belly of a plane. The noise was incredible, reminding me of those first post-CRISPR days when my head felt like it would burst. But after a while the air became thin and dry and cold again, like Cuenca, and I settled into an uneasy sleep.

I'll skip the transition through Customs and the trip to Charlie's house. Suffice it to say I was confused and withdrawn during the whole ordeal and for days afterwards.

Charlie's home was huge by Ecuadorian standards, though I gathered from comments he made on the phone to his friends and family that it was normal for the US. I disliked the laminate floors in the living area intensely, both for their plasticky odor and the way my toenails scraped on them, so I endeavored to spend as much time as I could on the kitchen tile or in the carpeted bedrooms.

But the wonderful thing about Charlie's American home was that it had a backyard that opened onto a power-line easement that stretched for miles! Several times a day, I'd stand by the back door.

"Run!" I'd say.

"You want to run? You want to run?" Charlie would reach for the doorknob. I'd obediently sit, quivering with anticipation.

"Stay!" he'd say, while he opened the door.

I'd freeze.

"Go, Mashi! Run!"

I'd dash out the door, pause to work the latch on the back gate, and race for miles up and down under the power lines. Sometimes I'd interact with people or animals. I'd meet a human jogger, try to herd a giggling group of children playing, or chase a cat briefly. I'd encounter other dogs and we'd exchange pleasantries, butt-sniff, play bow, and run back and forth a few times; as a herding breed, I wasn't as much of a pack animal as most dogs. But there are no words for the joy I felt in running as fast as I could, as far as I wanted. In those moments, I was free from the strangeness of the creature I'd become, no longer dog, not quite person.

I was free of the deception of pretending to be stupider than I am.

Finally, Charlie would put two fingers in his mouth and whistle. I might be a mile away by then, almost to the concrete wall atop which the interstate ran, but I'd hear, turn, and race back. I think those runs were all that saved me from losing my mind.

Charlie worked as an independent laboratory safety consultant (ironic, considering how many US regulations he'd violated by performing his CRISPR on me). He'd have various contracts around the Dallas area where we lived, often requiring him to go to work every day for weeks or months, but he was otherwise a solitary human. In his free time, he spoke with other humans mostly by phone.

In Ecuador, he'd been forced to venture into the mercados for food, he'd had a weekly card game with other English-speaking expats. He'd even had an Ecuadorian girlfriend, though her pregnancy (I could smell that the baby was his, but he didn't believe it, and I remained tactfully silent on the matter) and subsequent breakup was what precipitated our sudden move. But here, he ordered groceries and anything else he needed online, had a call girl in every couple of weeks, and spoke on the phone when he spoke to anyone at all.

Or, he spoke to me.

"Good boy, Mashi! Is he a good boy?"

"Goo(yip) oy!" I'd respond.

"Here's a cookie!" He'd give me a treat, one of the fishy, brothy tasting crisps I loved.

I realized what he was doing. *Two can play at that game,* I thought.

That day while he was at work, I dragged a runner from the carpeted bedroom to the detestable laminate floor. When Charlie came home, after he'd let me out for my run, I came home to find he'd moved the rug back where it had come from.

"Who's a good boy?" Charlie asked expectantly.

I stood looking at him, wagging my tail.

"Who's a *good boy*?" he asked, more slowly and loudly.

I clicked my poor toenails across that heinous laminate to the bedroom and stood, looking at him, next to the runner. He followed me.

"Who's a good boy?" He tried again. I slowly wagged my tail but didn't move, holding his gaze, summoning the alpha authority of my days as king of the mercado.

Slowly, it dawned on him. He picked up the runner and put it back roughly where I'd had it, forming a bridge across the clicky, smelly laminate so I could cross from carpet to tile without touching it. I marched proudly across the bridge and stood by my food bowl.

"Goo(yip) oy!" I proclaimed.

* * *

Training Charlie went well after that. Some things he knew I was teaching him to do, like leaving a few treats on the counter so I could help myself when he was at work.

"Treats." I pointed at the counter with my nose. Once he figured out what I wanted, he seemed amused. I rewarded him with a new vocabulary word each time.

"Chair," I'd say, hopping on and off the kitchen chair. "Ook," nudging an open book on the coffee table.

Other behaviors took longer to reinforce, because he had no idea he was doing them. Leaving his computer logged into voice command mode, for example. I had to wait for him to enable it, which he did only occasionally. That day I chattered my way through all my vocabulary words and tossed in a few new ones. It took three or four months of that, and about forty new words, before he started leaving voice command on all the time. After that, it took a number of redirection strategies before he got in the habit of leaving it on and walking away from it in the morning when he went to work.

Now I was cooking, as they say. Though, no, I never felt any urge to learn to cook. Dogs are almost without exception raw-foods enthusiasts. Cooking smells are just a signal to us that humans are handling food and we'd better get in there and get our share.

I did feel the urge to learn, though. And in an era of instant e-learning online, a talking dog with a voice-activated computer is all set. There was a bit of a learning curve on the computer's part while it learned to deal with my, shall we say, extremely idiosyncratic accent. And there was a panicked near-miss one time when the garage door opened and I almost didn't get the web browser shut down in time.

After that, I started a program of talking more immediately on his entry whenever he took a long time to get out of the car and come inside. That was such a subtle behavior to reinforce it took many months to have any noticeable effect on his transition time. After a year or so, though, he was consistently sitting in the car and sipping a beverage, flipping through social media on his phone, before coming inside. Much less stressful for me.

By the time I turned eight, I was talking with Charlie using the vocabulary of a bright three-year-old. I had finished 6th-grade math and introductory computer science, and worked my way, backwards, through world history to the 6th century on Chan Academy. I had several e-mail accounts. Being, as I mentioned, thumbless, I had to wait with vigilance and patience for Charlie to leave his credit card lying out, but by that time I had fairly good control over how much he drank each evening. So when he laid the card down by the keyboard and poured himself a scotch, it was a simple matter of tail wags, nudges, licks, a couple of new words, and so forth to lead him to drink seven or eight of them. He staggered to bed and fall in with his clothes on, so I dragged the quilt over him to make sure he'd sleep soundly. Then I went back and memorized the card information, front and back. I carefully replaced the card where he'd left it.

As I surfed online more, I began to look at Charlie's wardrobe critically. Though he had PhD in biochemistry, and seemed to have adequate clientele, I could tell that he was pushing the boundaries of acceptable attire: worn flip-flops, chinos that were faded and frayed, and as he spent more time in the USA, home of giant portions and sugary drinks and snacks, his polo shirts had begun to stretch across his belly unflatteringly. I burrowed into his closet and drawers, exhuming shirts in larger sizes, loafers, and dress socks, laboriously repacking his wardrobe so they were a little more accessible. Occasionally, I even dragged a particularly threadbare or tight garment out to the trash barrel on trash pick-up day when he was at work, though I risked one of the neighbors noticing and mentioning it to him. I logged onto his user accounts and searched for hours for business-casual clothing so he'd be inundated with ads for dressier trousers. His ad feed was now full of photos of men posing gazing off the pier in yachting clothes, or standing by a big desk in a corner office in crisp professional attire. Then, one night, I made a real sacrifice to achieve my goals: I chewed up his flip-flops.

I won't lie: I enjoyed it. I *am* a dog, and the combined flavors and aromas of leather, rubber, and toe jam were scrumptious. But, unlike stupider dogs, I fully understood that I would be scolded and punished for it. I may be a standoffish herding dog, but I *am* a dog, and being yelled at and having my nose smacked, followed by being locked in my crate, was an emotionally difficult experience for me even knowing that it was for a good cause. But my sacrifice was rewarded the next day when he finally donned the loafers that I'd tugged just far enough out of the back bottom corner of the closet so that he could spot them.

Now I had a master whose appearance I could at least be somewhat proud of, even if he was an unethical, awkward boor. It made me miss Hector even more: Hector, the butcher, the *don* of the mercado, a true *caballero*, respected by the *indigenas* in their velvet skirts, beloved by all the almond-eyed children, so respected he was sometimes asked to mediate petty disputes, always forthright, always upright, and always kind.

One day I was out on my run, closing in on the dull vehicular roar of the freeway embankment, when I caught the whiff of a bitch in heat. It had been a long time, and this one had a healthy, intoxicating aroma. My nose took over my body, my mind just along for the ride, and I veered to the smell's source.

Which was an eight-foot privacy fence segregating a yard from the power-line easement. For a dog of my agility, all it took was a running start. I leapt in the air, fully committed. My feet scrabbled up the top few feet of the fence, my momentum carrying me to the top. My front paws hooked over, my back claws dug in...and I was in the yard with a gorgeous female Rottweiler. It was one of the most joyous matings of my life. The Rottweiler's owner looked out her window just as we finished and came out, yelling, to chase me away. The human grabbed my paramour's collar, causing her sleek brown and black coat to ripple. I grinned and pressed myself against the gate, hoping to avoid any more unpleasantness. The human let go of the bitch and closed in on me.

"Smart one, aren't you?" she asked.

You have no idea! I thought.

She opened the latch and I was out before she could open the gate completely. I felt relaxed, invigorated, alive! It didn't even dull my mood when I heard Charlie's whistle

41

just at that moment. I contentedly turned my path towards his home.

Things went on this way for several more months. Charlie, with his improved image, got better clients and steadier work, and began to socialize a bit, leaving me at home for longer periods on weekend evenings. I progressed in my studies, but still I yearned for Hector. Then I reached the Chan Academy lessons on the Olmec and pre-contact Andean civilizations and my homesickness began to throb palpably.

It was then that I began to formulate a plan.

So, here I am. It turned out to be almost absurdly simple, really. I created an online account with a special service for exporting pets to foreign countries. After a thousand or so attempts, I held a pen in my mouth and forged my vet's signature on the required certificate of health. Today, the appointed pick-up date, I dragged my crate out onto the porch, stacked the paperwork neatly on a wicker loveseat, weighted it down with a rock, and climbed into the crate.

I'm sitting here waiting for the transport truck to pull up. The address for delivery is the butcher of the *mercado* on Calle Veintiocho de Febrero, Cuenca, Ecuador. My crate is to be released on the signature of one Hector.

And, to make my triumph complete, I can smell a litter of newborn, half-Rottweiler puppies on the breeze. Apparently, one of the amazing things about CRISPR is that it alters the germ line of future generations. If I'm not mistaken, the Rottweiler's mistress will be quite taken aback one day when she talks to the puppies.

And they talk back.

Contact

John Grey

Engrossed by sky glitter
from my first days,
what are the chances
that, out of numberless stars,
solar systems, galaxies,
there could be someone
as much as I am a someone,
even now,
headed this way,
with no other mission
than to make themselves
known to me,
that contact could happen
for the very first time
during my brief Earth sojourn,
two creatures
from opposite ends of the universe
standing face to face,
connecting, interacting,
my imagination's threads
becoming fabric in reality.

Puddle Duck
Priya Sridhar

It was a Friday night, and a busy shift. The delivery van reeked with old and new pizza. Ben sweated as he navigated another curve. He hadn't changed his work uniform, and the pizza boxes weren't strapped properly in the back. They slid and slipped behind him. He hoped that Garnet's pineapples didn't fall off her pizza.

He slowed down before another hairpin curve, the last before he reached his final delivery. That probably saved him. A flash of silver and something brown with long hair clomped onto the road.

Ben hit the brakes. He could feel the mud slipping beneath the wheels, and for a moment he panicked, The van screeched to a stop. He slowed just before the hairpin curve. The brown and silver flash whinnied.

It took a few minutes for Ben to move. He feared that outside meant he would step over the edge of the mountains and tumble into the darkness. The headlights remained on; Ben thanked God for that. He made sure to put on the parking brake before setting the windshield wipers at maximum. This allowed him to see what had nearly crashed into the van.

It looked like a muddy-brown horse wrapped in fishing line. Ben could see a large hook lodged in its mouth, the kind of hook you'd see at a fishing wharf. The fishing line cut into its neck and bloodied mane. The horse had sharp teeth, which gleamed in the glow of his headlights.

Ben sucked in his breath. He pressed his hand to the rune stone. He had seen his fair share of horses, from his grandparents' farm. He knew that horses had flat teeth and thin eyelashes. This one looked like a brown, hairy dinosaur with thick, reptilian skin around its eyes.

The creature locked eyes with him. Although every instinct told him to hit the gas pedal and go the other way, a small part of him saw the frothing fear. This creature needed help, and it needed his help. The pendant he wore under his Infinity Pizza shirt warmed.

Thing is, he didn't know how to help a horse like this. But someone he knew did.

*   *   *

Garnet waited on the porch, in a white rocking chair. She was a tall woman with pepper-gray corkscrew curls, glasses that made her look like an owl, and a billowing yellow dress embroidered with tiny white carnations. She was combing her hair with one hand and holding a radio in the other. Jimi Hendrix's "May This Be Love" crooned against the pouring rain.

"Ben," she said, as he straggled up the path to her porch, sliding on the smooth pebbles she had carefully arranged. "Is everything alright?"

"Can you tell me?" He panted, as he dropped pieces of pineapple pizza. "I'm sorry about your order."

She saw. The giant creature that was following nibbled at each torn piece. Garnet marveled at how the horse could eat with the giant hook in its mouth. She also felt fear on seeing how close Ben was to it.

"Ben, that's a kelpie."

"A what?" He shivered with the rain.

"A man-eating horse."

"WHAT?"

"Come close to me. Don't make sudden movements."

Ben obeyed. He stumbled over the slippery stone path, trying not to startle the creature. Garnet put down the radio and walked toward him. The kelpie's ears weren't flattened, but it was distracted. Also, it was far from the water.

"Get behind me," she ordered when she was close enough.

Ben slid behind her. Garnet took the pizza box from him. She laid it on the ground, never taking her eyes off the sharp-toothed, distressed creature.

"I've never seen one before," she said. "My Scottish grandfather mentioned taming one as a plough horse in the old country. But we're not in the old country."

"What do you mean?" Ben whispered.

"He'd have used a bridle with a cross etched on it to tame one," Garnet explained. "But I don't keep any bridles

45

here, and I don't believe in the cross. It doesn't work if you refuse to believe."

"I was raised by Unitarians," Ben offered.

"That doesn't count; you're not a witch."

"What do we do then?"

"I believe in other things," Garnet said. "Go on into the house. There should be towels for you to dry off. Get a pair of wire-cutters from the toolbox in the kitchen, and a flashlight."

He trudged inside, rainwater dripping off his curls and clothes. Garnet knelt by the kelpie, her eyes darting to the ground. The downpour soaked through her thin yellow dress and through her carefully sculpted curls. She picked up a tiny pebble coated in mud.

"I hope this works," she told the creature. "If it doesn't, please don't eat my hand."

Using the mud, she drew a peace symbol on the pizza box. The kelpie kept eating and whining in pain. Garnet finished the symbol. The great creature lay on the ground gently.

Ben returned with two towels, the flashlight, a coil of rope, and the wire cutters. He had wrapped himself in a thick blue towel and wrapped another one around Garnet's shoulders. She offered him a grateful smile through the downpour.

"I'm going to cut off the fishing line first," she said. "For the hook we'll have to hold its jaws open, and I'd rather not tackle that until the rest of it is free."

Ben's damp face paled, but he didn't object. Garnet took the black wire cutters and carefully navigated herself around the kelpie. She wrapped the towel tighter around her shoulders.

"Shine the flashlight here," she called. "I need to see where the fishing line is."

The yellow, heavy-duty light clicked; a gleam shone over the silky, quivering horsehair. Garnet traced a silver line along the kelpie's flank. She slid the wire cutters under it and snipped. Then she leaned back quickly. The kelpie kept its head buried in the pizza box.

It took two hours for her to untangle the rest of the line. While the kelpie was surprisingly docile, especially after she

46

looped the rope around its neck and painted a peace sign on the coarse thread, it did twitch. Garnet had to locate each fine strand, and untangle it. Red lines streaked the poor creature's body, sometimes with tiny cuts. The bloodstained threads lay among the stone pebbles in a neat pile. Ben cursed when he saw how the kelpie twitched from the pain.

"What happened to it?" he asked.

"I don't know," Garnet said. "If I didn't know any better, I'd say someone tried to catch it using a fishing rod and managed to hook it."

"You can't catch anything that big with a fishing pole! Who would be that stupid?"

"You'd be surprised," she replied. "Now for the hard part; we have to get that hook out. It's too thick for me to cut out the barb, and those are sharp teeth."

Ben nodded. He shined the flashlight over the affected area. The hook had thick flecks of red rust, and had maybe moved an inch as Garnet had removed the fishing line. It remained lodged in the kelpie's lower jaw. Garnet pondered the gleaming sharp object.

"We'll use the wire cutters to pull it out," Ben said. "Neither of us wants to lose a hand, so we need something that can hold onto the hook."

Garnet nodded. She peered at the hook, and used the wire cutters to hold it tight. Ben kept shining the flashlight and grabbed the other end of the rope. His arms felt too skinny in case the creature went berserk and tried to canter off, but he had to try.

"I have one chance," she said. "I'm so sorry about this, love."

"Don't apologize," Ben said. "I brought him to you."

"I was talking to the kelpie." Garnet gave a nervous smile. "She must be as scared as we are."

"*She?*"

"On three, Ben. One, two . . . three!"

The hook came out in one swoop. A piercing wail cut between them and the kelpie's head shot up despite the rope around its neck. The rope burned Ben's hands as brown hair slapped his face. Sharp teeth connected with one of his arms, making him drop the flashlight. It clattered on the ground. Shard of the yellow beam shone against the thrashing kelpie. He felt blood run down his arm.

"Ben!" Garnet grabbed him by his uninjured arm and pulled him away. They stumbled back onto the porch, out of the rain. For a few moments they watched. The kelpie stumbled to its feet and ran. It left behind the hook and the pile of fishing line. The galloping hoof steps faded.

"I'm okay." Ben held up his arm to the porch light. The gash was curved. "It's not too deep."

"It needs stitches." Garnet's voice was firm. "Fortunately I can help with that. Let's get the first-aid kit."

They went into her kitchen, a chamber with wallpaper of the planets on each of the walls. Garnet reached into a cupboard with warped wood. She brought out a dented metal first-aid kit, which had several large suture needles and bandages. Ben stared at the needles.

"I could drive to the hospital . . ." he started.

"Nonsense. The roads are practically watered out and they wouldn't treat you well."

"I wouldn't say that-"

"Your binder is loose." Garnet indicated at her chest. "I think I would say that. They would notice and call you 'Joanna' or 'Joan'."

Ben looked down and blushed. The rain had soaked through his shirt and the binder under it.

"My dead name was Jeanne," he said in a meek voice.

Garnet opened a jar of a strange, minty substance. She spread it on Ben's gash. The turquoise gel numbed the stinging sensation, and stopped the blood. Although he winced when she wiped antiseptic over a large needle and threaded it, he didn't move as she pierced the skin.

"You're lucky," she said.

"I know," he replied. "One horse I knew nearly bit off my grandfather's shoulder. And that was an ordinary horse."

"You should spend the night. It's not safe, with that kelpie out there and with the rain."

"What about my other deliveries? I don't want to lose my job . . ."

"Leave that to me," she said. "You know I'm good with keeping you employed."

48

Her eyes went to a toothbrush that was in the first-aid kit, and some short green feathers. Ben looked at it with confusion.

"Where do you think it went?" he asked when she finished stitching him up.

"To find water," Garnet replied. "She needs to find a body of water where she will recover. I hope we never see her again."

"How do you know it was a . . ." Ben felt his face growing hot again.

"I took a glance while cutting the fishing line." Garnet's voice remained prim. "Kelpies have similar bodies to horses, after all."

"Oh . . ."

"You can wash up in my bathroom. I don't have clothes that fit, but there should be a robe."

Ben nodded. The gel and stitches together felt odd, since he couldn't feel the twinges of pain. It would hurt later. He couldn't bring himself to worry.

*   *   *

The sunlight through a dirty window woke him up. Ben's eyes blinked. He studied the robe he was wrapped in: black wool embroidered with large golden hibiscus flowers. The golden, satin flowers were stiff and scratched his finger when he pressed it. He groaned and stretched out of bed. The stitches on his arm ached. Under his robe, new bandages replaced the old ones.

The smell of coffee and freshly made toast made his stomach rumble. Ben got out of bed and registered the room. It had walls covered in white and green stripes, and shelves made of driftwood. A knickknack of a three-headed dog crouched in a playful pose, mouth open for a bone. Ben stroked its back. The carved wood was warm to the touch.

"Oh drat," Garnet said from outside, voice muffled through the door. "She's still here."

Ben wrapped the robe tighter around his middle and joined her outside on the porch. She sipped coffee from a chipped lavender mug. The rain last night had ruined her curls, so that they were lopsided and dangling from her left side entirely. Some curls clung to her left cheek, which she

49

didn't bother to brush away. She was wearing a bright aqua dressing gown, which seemed to be made of wool.

"Good morning, Garnet," he told her.

"Good morning, Ben." She took a slow sip. "There's breakfast in the kitchen if you need it."

"I should hit the road," he said as his stomach rumbled. "My boss is going to kill me."

"Don't worry," she told him. "A lot of people last night remember the rain knocking out their phones, and they swear that they weren't able to get their orders through. Including me. Your boss gave you the night off and told you to go home."

"How?" he asked.

"Suggestions," she answered. "You just suggest to people the explanation they want, after you reach into their collective subconscious, and they grab onto it."

He noted the dark circles under her eyes, and her disheveled curls. Her bare feet were flecked with mud and various scratches; Ben could picture her romping on the stone path out in the rain, wearing her worn slippers, reaching the main road, and avoiding cars. She would do that, to reach each house and make suggestions to each customer. Ben remembered Garnet doing that once, when he had broken his leg chasing pixies off her property.

"I'm sorry," he said. "I brought the kelpie to you. I didn't know what else to do."

"Don't be sorry," she said. "What if it had eaten someone else while flailing with a hook in its mouth? What if the fisherman that tried to catch it came to finish the job? You did the right thing, Ben. Your clothes are drying on the line, by the way. We'll have to replace the binder so that no one notices. I can sew it up, or make a new one."

"Thank you," he said. "What did you mean by 'she's still here?'?"

"Take a look at my pond." She pointed. "It took me several years of hatching tadpoles and luring water birds to make it nice and neat."

"You . . . use frogs and birds in . . . potions?"

"I like watching them," she said simply. "Some frogs are poisonous, you know. It's best to just let them grow."

She walked out onto the stones. He followed, his head aching. He saw the kelpie's head poking out from the pond. Tiny bones littered the rim of the pool, as did feathers and blue fish tails.

"It's still here," he said in disbelief.

"She is," Garnet agreed with disgust. "Closest body of water, and filled with enough food to keep her happy for a day. I'm going to see if I can take her rope off, so she can go and leave us in peace. It's going to take me years to redo my pond."

She trudged forward. Ben followed, with reluctance. He saw the rope, slippery and slimy, and still looped around the kelpie's neck. It gave him a beady-eyed stare. Ben stepped back.

"Um, hi," he said. "You remember me? Weird night, huh?"

The frilly eyes didn't leave his face. Ben froze as it shook slimy water out of its mane and clambered out of the water. Garnet approached it, making sure she was slow.

"Easy, girl," she said. "We know you don't want to be here. I know I don't want you to be here. Just need to get that rope off and you can go on your way and eat a random cow."

She grabbed the end of the rope and started to ease it off the kelpie. The water had made the rope thinner and tighter. Still, the kelpie didn't resist. Garnet managed to get the entire rope off and toss it at a distance. Tiny strands of rope clung to her hands.

"Okay, you're free now," she said. "Come on, girl. Get on with it."

The kelpie switched its beady-eyed look to her. She locked eyes with it.

"It can't be the pizza," she said. "That bind was meant to be temporary. You're not staying here."

Neither of them blinked. Ben didn't move. He watched with fascination.

The kelpie slowly clambered, one hoof at a time. It shook its mane, spraying the grass with pond slime and frog guts. Then it walked towards them.

"You're free," Garnet repeated. "Go. Bug off, girl. We don't want you here."

51

"Careful, Garnet," Ben said.

The kelpie came up towards them, turning its head. Then it breathed into their faces. Ben coughed as he inhaled the strong rotten frog scent. Garnet turned her head away, clenching her coffee mug. The kelpie's lips pressed to Ben's injured arm.

"Hey!" Ben tried to jump back, but he felt no connecting teeth. When he tried to walk back, the kelpie moved closer towards him. It matched his steps. When he tried to step further back, it wrapped its neck around him. The warm fur felt warm and sizzling against the cool morning.

"What's she doing?" Garnet asked, spilling some of her coffee in trying to get between the kelpie and Ben. She wasn't successful, however; the kelpie put its brown, sleek body between the two of them. When she tried to walk around it, the kelpie curled around Ben.

"Horses do this when they like someone," Ben said, feeling the rubbery lips on thin neck. "They nuzzle, or lip you when they want to show affection.

"Oh no," she said with horror.

"Oh yes," Ben replied grimly. "This kelpie likes us."

*   *   *

Ben left for his day shift, after making sure that the kelpie wouldn't eat Garnet and that it stopped nuzzling him. The kelpie nickered at him to stay. Despite himself, Ben rubbed its neck with hesitation.

"I gotta go, girl," he said. "Work's a-calling. You should run off to your home, shouldn't you?"

The kelpie seemed to understand that he had to leave. But it gave one last protesting nicker.

Ben got to work half an hour early. The boss told him to wash dishes and help with the dough, but that until the phone lines were repaired, and most likely no one would be ordering pizza that evening. It would mean docked pay, but Ben didn't mind. The kelpie worried him. Money was money, but he didn't want a savage horse chewing on Garnet.

By evening, and by the time Ben returned, Garnet's hair was tangled and sweaty, and her face betrayed frustration. She told him that she did all she could to get the kelpie to leave. She sprinkled various herbs into the pond. Her

52

fingers traced banishing runes into the muddy banks. Garnet even pulled out a frozen chicken from her pantry and tried to lure it out. In response, the fanged creature rubbed its head into her shoulder. Then it made a beeline for the chicken, swallowed it in three bites, and returned to the pond.

"I can't have a kelpie for a pet!" she said to Ben. "She's too big! She's too boisterous! And she eats people!"

They were drinking iced tea. Ben had brought two pizzas from work, leftovers mainly. The kelpie remained in the pond.

"But we can't make her leave," Ben mused. "You've tried everything!"

"Urgh." Garnet massaged her forehead. "I can't do this."

They heard the kelpie stepping out of the pond. Brown fur shook out droplets of water and blood.

"Oh no, you're still bleeding," Garnet said with dismay as the kelpie trotted to them on the porch and lay her head in Ben's lap. Her tongue lapped at the pizza on a nearby plate.

"Oof, watch it." Ben stroked the kelpie's head and winced at the blood droplets. "Now you're being all sweet."

"She still needs to heal." Garnet put down her iced tea and tentatively offered her hand. "I guess she can stay until she's healthy enough to live on her own."

"Should we name her then? At least so that we have something to call her besides 'kelpie'?"

"If we have to, she needs a name that won't get us attached. Like Pondweed or Mud Scum."

"Puddle Duck," Ben suggested. "I don't like ducks that much."

"Neither do I. And she's not anything like a duck." Garnet's strokes became gentler. "But a name that means she's leaving. So Puddle Duck it is. I hope it means that she finds a new pond soon."

Ben's stitches tingled. They told him it wouldn't be a short-term deal. The way Puddle Duck dozed on his lap, like she hadn't bitten into him only the previous night, also notified him that she was staying. Puddle Duck was theirs, for better or for worse.

Nightingale's Song
J.A. Prentice

Over the flat blue of the Summer Sea rose an isle of white cliffs and green hills, surrounded by spires of stone where seagulls dived low over gleaming waters.

Upon the cliffs a woman walked: hair black as night, skin fair as moonlight, dress white as lily's petals. Around her neck hung a chain of twisted bronze. A crown of flowers was woven into her deep black hair.

As she walked, the mournful maiden sang. Any who heard her would have been moved to tears, but only sky and sea were witness.

"Woe! Woe! For my sisters three
Boldest was Faeda
Dawn's gleaming sword
Mightiest was Maeda
Midday's heavy mace
Wisest was Kaeda
Twilight's secret spell
And I by the hearth
Soft Naeda Nightingale
Songstress and fourth
Through the night
The long watch I kept
From sundown to sunrise
While still they slept
Woe! Woe! That ever they trusted me.

Woe! Woe! I did not keep my vigil!
On ship black as despair
The beast-man came upon
The shores of my isle fair
And bound my sisters with spell and sigil.

Woe! For shining Faeda
Woe! For bold Maeda

Woe! For wise Kaeda
And woe to me
Naeda Doom-Bringer
I did not keep my watch
Naeda Cliff-Singer
I did not keep the vigil."

Each day she walked the cliffs till her fair feet blistered red. Then back down she went, head held low, chains trailing behind her like snakes in the long grass.

Over waters dark and bright, under cloud and sun, Hamus dae Neithan sailed south in his small boat, the wide sail full of strong wind. He stood upon the prow, watching the sea stream past. Under a sash of checkered green and black, he wore a dark tunic. Around his neck hung a pendant of winding roots, fashioned from shining silver. The hilt of his sword was like a horned beast, eyes made of tiny pearls.

These were the last worldly possessions he had. All else had slipped away in fire and blood.

He sat and marked his sheepskin chart. Running his fingers over his jaw, he felt faint scars and wiry hair. His amber eyes swam with smothering shadows and his tawny skin was burned dark by the sun.

He never looked north. To look back would be to remember his proud father cut down by a blow to the throat, his brave sister hoisted high upon the old tree, and his noble mother destroyed by despair and a leap from the battlements.

Revenge no longer weighed upon his thoughts. The fire in his heart had burnt out, leaving nothing but cold ash.

Clan Neithan was no more. All that remained was a mariner upon a lonely sea.

****

Oppressive darkness pushed Naeda from all sides. Rotten animal stench smothered her. The foul warmth of sweat and spoiling meat filled the beast's den. Her chains trailed in the muck, bronze eels lurking beneath murky waters.

"Naeda!"

55

The voice boomed, accompanied by a reeking gust of blazing breath.

"Naeda!"

Naeda sank to her knees before the hulking shape of her master. Brown and red stained her lily-white dress. With black eyes downcast, she spoke.

"What do you want, master and chain-maker?"

Her master leaned forward and let out another noxious breath.

"Sing for me," he ordered. "Sing."

Naeda nodded and summoned all her strength to sing in this foulest of foul places. A low hum slipped from between her quivering lips and he cackled.

"Sing!" he roared. "Sing!"

With trembling voice, Naeda sang of how winter and summer were lovers doomed never to meet, of how flowers were the youthful dead stolen before their time, and of how the sea was filled by the tears of the giantess Glenlaeth when she saw her father had been slain and his bones fashioned into white isles.

For each verse she shed a tear; for each story she let out a shaking cry.

When her song of the shepherd who lost his way turned to gasping sobs, her master clapped his hands together and laughed.

"No more, Night-watcher. You have earned the right to breathe another day."

Naeda curtseyed as though he were a fair elven king, let out a swift, "Thank you, my master," and fled fast as she could, the animal roar of his laughter chasing her. She stumbled over hills until she came to a bright spring of fresh water. Casting her dress aside, she bathed to wash away the stench that had soaked into her skin.

Her tears echoed soft through empty hills.

Hamus's food was long gone and little more than a drop of fresh water remained in his flask. With each passing moment, the waves looked more appealing. He knew the water could not be drunk, yet his parched throat begged him to try.

56

He considered his sword: a swift end, more merciful than the slow torment of sea and sun as his body failed.

Then he saw a thin sliver of white and green upon the horizon. He cheered as he realized what they were. Just a little ahead of him were cliffs and hills, rocks and grass and trees and streams. Land loomed just within his reach.

Upon the prow he perched, letting the breeze stir his dark, untamed mane, eyes fixed upon the approaching isle.

Naeda stood upon the cliff, watching waves grind relentlessly at pale chalk.

What would happen, she wondered, *if the cliff gave way and I fell under the churning waves? Would these chains slip from my bones?*

She listened to the cry of a seagull. Over rock and sea it flew, feathers orange-red in the dying light.

Naeda sang. With each word, she stepped forward, ready at last to sing no more.

Hamus sat up as if pulled by a string. A soft voice sang, borne upon the wind. He stood and looked across the sea. At the top of a high cliff was a woman, like a lily in the green grass.

"Woe! Woe!" the songstress sang. "*For my sisters three.*"

All other thoughts faded from Hamus's mind. He felt the weight upon his heart lift – not because the song was joyful, but because it was sad. It was a song that felt as he felt, a sorrow like his own.

And as lonely boat drifted closer to lonely isle, he felt he was not alone.

"*Woe to Faeda!*" Naeda sung, centimeters from the ledge. "*Woe to Maeda!*"

Her breathing was steady, her heart still. She missed not a single note of her song.

"*Woe to Kaeda!*" the woman sang and Hamus realized how close she was to the cliff edge.

"*Woe to me!*" Naeda sang. "*Naeda doom-bringer!*"

The sea breeze tickled her toes. The tiniest step and the ocean would swallow her whole.

"Prisoner of the beast! Cliff-singer."

She sang so low it was almost a whisper.

"I did not keep my vigil."

Hamus was close enough to see her face. What he saw written there he knew too well, as if it were a dark mirror.

"No!" he cried. "Stop!"

Naeda opened her eyes and laughed with delight. Here was hope, hope at last – a visitor borne across the sea.

Chalk crumbled under her feet and she fell.

Throwing off sash and sword, Hamus leapt into the cold bay after Naeda. Water pounded him, but his arms were strong. She was tossed by the waves, white dress turned ghostly by the water, black hair falling across her frozen features.

Hamus grabbed hold of her, lifting her above the waves. Her eyes flashed open and she gasped, clinging tight to him. His tunic was soaked through, dragging him down as he struggled back to the boat. Cold waves stung his eyes, filling his nose and mouth. The roar of water was all he could hear.

At last, he grabbed hold of the boat and shouted at Naeda to climb aboard. She nodded, hair dripping, and clambered in. Hamus leapt after her, landing in a splash of frigid seawater.

Naeda was trying to say something, but Hamus couldn't hear over the thundering of the waves. He took hold of the oar, pulling the boat towards a nearby strip of beach where sand and rounded pebbles mingled with the tide. A moment later he was hauling the boat ashore, the woman hurrying to give him a hand.

"I'm sorry," she said as Hamus collapsed on the sand.

"Don't worry about it," Hamus grunted. "Just tell me you aren't a mirage."

Naeda touched her hand to his face, fingers trailing over his beard like raindrops.

"Not a mirage," she whispered.

"Good," Hamus replied. "It would have been stupid to almost drown for a mirage."

"I'm Naeda."

"I know," Hamus said. "From the song."

"You heard it?"

"Aye. Most of it." He coughed, globs of saltwater rising from his throat. "But do you mind if we discuss your music when we aren't freezing to death?"

"Of course." Naeda looked around. "We'll need a fire."

"Flint," Hamus grunted.

"What?" Naeda asked.

"Flint!" Hamus pointed to some pale stones just behind her.

"Oh!" Naeda cried.

Hamus tore a plank of wood from the deck of his boat. "Firewood."

"Or..." Naeda pointed at a tree sprouting from the cliff. "We could just use some of those branches."

Scarlet sunlight scattered through the clouds, painting the sky shades of red, orange, and violet, as the two sat by their growing fire. Shivering, Hamus ripped off his water-logged tunic and threw it by the fire. Naeda's eyes went wide.

"What's the matter?" Hamus asked. "Don't have men where you come from?"

"No. Not except–"

Her voice trailed off and she shook like a reed hut facing the ocean wind.

"Take off your dress," Hamus said.

Naeda started. "What?"

"You'll freeze to death."

Naeda paused, eyes full of shadows.

"I'll turn around," Hamus promised.

She pulled off the soaked white cloth the moment his back was turned. Cold wind blew over her wet skin.

"Here." Without looking at her, Hamus pulled down the sail from the boat and flung it to her. "Wrap yourself up. Keep warm."

"What about you?"

Hamus shrugged. "I'm a big lad. I'll cope."

They huddled close as the flames climbed into the sky, a billowing tower of black smoke birthed from the purple-orange tip of the fire. Glad of the warmth, neither spared a thought for who else might see the plume of smoke or smell the ash upon the night air.

****

Deep in his foul den, the beast-man shifted in his sleep. A stream of dark smoke drifted over filth and debris, mingling with a thousand foul smells before it reached his large nostrils.

He snorted. His eyes opened, glowing like wildfire on a moonless night, and he let out a great bellow. Earth shook and stone shifted. The isle and the sea quaked in fear.

The beast-man was coming.

****

The cliff trembled. Chalk fell away, splashing into the waters, which churned as if caught in a storm. Seagulls took to the sky, shill cries deafening.

Naeda leapt, clutching the sail tight over her chest. Sweat drenched her white brow. Hamus stumbled to his feet, reaching for tunic and sword. Breathing heavily, he stood, staring into the night.

Nothing came. The bellow became an echo, then silence.

Hamus swore. "What manner of beast was that?"

"It is he," Naeda whispered. "My master. My sisters and I were keepers here. We watched for the beast-man's coming. They were watchers of morn, noon, and eve, whilst I sung through the long night." She hung her head. "But I fell asleep. And he came." The memories hovered in her eyes like ghosts. "My sisters he bound in their sleep so they would not wake. He bound me as well."

She stretched out her wrists, chains gleaming in the moonlight.

"The brute." Hamus gripped his sword tight. "Can't you wake your sisters?"

Naeda shook her head. "He worked magic too deep. It must be pierced with a three-fold spell: tears of the mourner, silver stained with sorrow–"

"You'd be a mourner, wouldn't you?" Hamus interrupted.

Naeda nodded. "Aye."

60

"And this..." Hamus pulled the necklace from where it sat on his chest. "This has seen sorrow enough for any spell."

Naeda took it and wrapped it in her pale fingers. A mournful song escaped her lips, a wordless whisper of lament, like the music of a songbird downed by a broken wing.

"Aye." She brushed the tears from his bearded cheek. "There is sorrow enough."

Hamus looked at her – the tears in her eyes, the chains on her wrists – and embraced her. She buried her face in his chest.

They parted and Naeda smiled her first smile since the night her sisters had fallen into slumber. Her lips parted and she let out two notes, sweeter than any lyre.

In those notes were the bonds of shared sorrow, the compassion of one broken creature for another, the reaching of two hands across a dark and starless night.

So powerful were those notes that Hamus knew that for her, he would brave fire and storm. He would walk the frozen north and sail the long sea. He would face dragon and djinn for nothing but her smile.

"Your music," he asked, "is it magic?"

She laughed and her laughter was as song also, dancing like a butterfly. Hamus smiled.

"All music is magic," she said. "For what is magic but the ability to make something from nothing? When the land was young, a single thought could move mountains. Now my song is less, but it is still magic."

With glinting eyes, she drew him in for a kiss. Though he said nothing, Hamus thought that must be magic too.

When at last their lips parted, he said, "the third thing?"

"Hmm?" Naeda asked, leaning in for another kiss.

"Threefold," he said, many minutes later. "Tears are one; silver is another; what's the third thing?"

"A blade," Naeda said.

Hamus laughed, picking up his blade and swinging it before her.

"A blade? Is that all? Then here!" He thrust the hilt at her. "Take it and let us be done with this beast!"

"A blade," Naeda replied, "bathed in beast-man's black blood."

The smile dropped from Hamus's face.

"Ach." He shook his head. "There's always a catch."

****

In his den, the beast-man sat on a throne of crimson-stained bones. Flies and maggots buzzed around him, a court of carrion-feeders. He breathed out a cloud of black breath, hot and rotten, like meat spoiling in the open. Black, red, and brown stains clung to his yellowed teeth.

For a moment, he considered going to deal with the newcomer who smelled of sweat and tears.

No, he decided, leaning back onto his death-throne. *Let him come to me.*

****

Over hill and ditch Naeda led Hamus, her hand never leaving his. All around were the skeletal trunks of leafless trees and patches of yellow, faded grass. Sunrise cast all in hues of blood and fire. Shadows shifted, each one sending a nervous twinge down Hamus's spine. He kept his hand tight upon his blade's hilt.

"Stay your fear," Naeda said. "The beast is not yet abroad."

"How can you be so sure?" Hamus asked.

"He casts shadow and scent wherever he goes," Naeda replied. "He is a lumberer, a stumbler. He moves as the charging boar and not as the butterfly."

"And how do we move?"

"I move as Nightingale," she said. "Swift and songful. And you... Perhaps the horse. Strong and yet graceful."

For her, Hamus thought, *I'd be proud stag or humble squirrel.*

Naeda drew to a halt as an old spring bubbled before them, its water coming out brown and black. Around the spring sprouted three trees. Each was withered, limbs stripped bare as bone. Black fungus crawled up the bark.

"There." Naeda pointed to the roots. "They sleep there."

Wrapped in the roots like slaves tangled in bonds were three women, proud faces set in restless sleep.

The first had hair of fiery orange and features fierce as a lion's.

62

"Here lies shining Faeda," sang Naeda.
"Dawn keeper!
Eldest and fairest."

Next Hamus came to a woman with hair like spun gold. There was joy in her face that even nightmares could not dissolve.

"Here lies bold Maeda
Midday warrior!
Bravest and brightest."

The last was solemner than the other two, with thin lips, pursed as if in thought. Silver hair hung over her face, gleaming despite the dirt.

"And last wise Kaeda
Twilight's watcher.
Darkest and wisest.
Woe, oh Woe!
To my sisters three
Who slumber here in shadow."

"They're beautiful," Hamus said, before hurriedly adding, "but not as beautiful as you."

"Aye." Naeda nodded. "They are. More beautiful than flower and field and sea."

Hamus took her hands and looked into her eyes.

"We will wake them," he vowed. "This blade will be painted in the beast's blood before the sun sets tonight."

Naeda shook her head. "It is no use! You will die in his den and he will feast upon your bones. What then will be gained? Naught but fresh sorrow to compound old."

"Then we take to my boat and sail until we find new land," he said, "with all our sorrows behind us."

Naeda hesitated, then tore away from him. She paced, winding in circles, a bird in a cage. At last she smiled a sad, dim smile.

"This was my temptation," she said. "A chance to be free. But I am Naeda Nightingale, songstress and watch-keeper. I cannot let my sisters remain while I go. I must endure the long night, as is my duty. But not yours, Hamus. Run before he catches your scent."

After a moment's silence, Hamus spoke. "My family is gone. My home is gone. I carry them with me, black ghosts and whispers in the dark. That's all I have left." He looked

63

at the sleeping faces of the sisters, buried in roots and dirt and shadows. "I can't bring back my family, but I can help you save yours. And maybe that might be enough."

Naeda's eyes glinted like dark seas. "Then we fight together."

Hamus drew his blade. "Let's end the night in bloody dawn. Either we fall or he does."

Naeda sang.

"Blade to be blooded
Dawn to be dreaded
Destiny falls
For good or for ill."

****

The den's maw gaped amidst fungus, mud, and scattered bones. A dark curtain of flies and maggots buzzed across it. Their legs brushed against Hamus's skin as though they were trying to see how his bones would taste.

Hamus took a deep breath and thought instead of Naeda's deep eyes, of Naeda's soft smile, of Naeda's sweet song, of Naeda's lips pressed against his.

That memory in his heart and his blade in his hand, Hamus strode to the threshold of the den, where fly-coated bones crunched in dark mud.

"Come forth, beast-man!" Hamus roared. "Come and feel the kiss of my blade. She does not spare her lovers!"

A low growl came from deep in the cave. Bones shook under Hamus's feet.

"You come here and make threats?" The voice sounded as if it came from a throat full of crushed skulls. "Man of soft flesh and weak bones, I will feast upon your marrow! This is my isle, marked in scent and spell and sigil. He who challenges me for it shall feel my teeth upon his throat!"

"Come forth," said Hamus, "and we shall see."

There came a rustle of movement like autumn winds stirring dry leaves, then footsteps like spring thunder. Hamus stepped back, sword raised.

A retching stench of decay announced the beast-man like trumpets at a parade. It was. Hamus nearly gagged.

Black insects spilled from the den – courtiers preceding their monarch. Nothing could be heard but their endless droning.

Then came the shadow amidst shadows, looming over Hamus like Sun's first rays over fleeing Moon.

Tall as a tree, jaw bloodstained, tusks like a wild boar, hairy as a mountain goat, naked as newborn babe, the beast-man stood upon the threshold of his den.

"You are foolish," the beast-man growled. "A mouse challenging the king of cats. I am blood and death and tusk and sinew. What are you?"

"Just a lad who saved a singing lass from drowning," Hamus said. "Hamus dae Neithan at your service."

"You know this is no fair challenge."

"Of course." Hamus grinned like a child with a sweet. "*I* have a sword."

A mass of muscle, fur, and fury, the beast-man charged. Hamus cried out as the weight knocked him back.

The beast-man came at him claw and tusk, cutting, biting, scarring. Hamus barely pulled away, covered in scarlet scratches.

With a snort of hot air, the beast-man charged again. Hamus dove to one side, swinging his blade. The edge caught the beast-man's arm, cutting through tangles of black fur and piercing odious flesh. Black blood oozed – a few drops, nothing more.

Hamus smiled and vaulted across the muddy earth.

A deep guffaw issued from snout-like lips.

"Run!" the beast-man roared. "Run, weak flesh and small teeth! Run, stinging sword! I will catch you! I will taste your blood on my tongue. I will make music of your death scream."

He dropped to all fours, charging after Hamus. Hamus remembered Naeda's song and ran faster, tearing through grass and mud with long strides, never looking back at the snarling shadow behind him.
****

Naeda's heart leapt as she spied Hamus racing towards her, her master close behind. Hamus was wounded, trailing red across brown earth.

Her tears had been shed into the spring and the silver cast upon it. All that remained was the blade in Hamus's hand, the blood gleaming like black ink in torchlight.

Less than a hundred yards away, Hamus stumbled, a snaking root catching his toe.

Naeda shrieked as the beast-man's tusks ripped into Hamus's side. Hamus fell, the sword still clutched tight. Blood came in torrents from his wound. The beast-man circled, growling.

"No!" Naeda cried.

The beast-man looked at her. The snarling features turned to mocking cruelty.

"What will you do, little Nightingale? You sing. Nothing more."

"Yes," Naeda replied. "I sing."

And she sang. The sound, deep and sorrowful, full of pain and loss but tinged also with hope, issued from her lips.

The beast-man roared, hands clapped to his ears. Blood dripped from his nose.

Hamus struggled to his feet. One hand held his sword; the other he pressed against his wound.

He ran, ignoring the pain, ignoring the beast-man, ignoring the hot liquid oozing down his side. He darted past Naeda and fell by the tainted spring. The sword dropped from his fingers. Black blood trickled into the foul waters.

The beast-man let out a roar, turned his savage eyes to Naeda, and rushed towards her. She did not flinch.

"I am Naeda Nightingale of the four sisters," she whispered. "I have sung my song and kept watch over my sisters as they sleep. I have held back the dark."

Hamus fell forward into dry grass. His eyes closed and he thought he heard golden horns calling across the long night.

Roots snapped; trees quaked; earth shivered.

They sprang up, three warriors blazing bright as stars. The beast-man stopped his charge and whimpered like a wounded wolf pup.

Naeda saw them and let loose a cry worthy of the heavens.

"My sisters!" she shouted. "I'm sorry!"

Faeda placed her hand on her younger sister's shoulder and smiled. "It's all right, Naeda."

"You kept the watch in the end," Kaeda whispered.

"And there's nothing like a fight in the early morning," Maeda said, swinging her gleaming mace.

Naeda watched as her sisters descended upon the quivering beast-man like birds-of-prey upon a mouse. His might was nothing against them. There was a crash of light and sound and song. Then the three stood back.

A small marker stood in the grass, a carved totem of a hairy, tusked man.

"He is back where he should be," Kaeda said.

"Pity it was over so fast," Maeda replied. "I'd have liked more of a challenge."

"You're back." Naeda embraced each of them in turn. "You're back!"

Kaeda held aloft the dark and twisted idol. "The beast-man is only fury and cruelty, an elder thing of carnage and blood. You are Naeda Nightingale. He could not stand for long against you."

"Not me alone," Naeda admitted. "It was Hamus who–"

Her face grew pale.

"Hamus!"

Bare feet pounding through bloodstained grass and mud, she raced to the spring. The water was running purer now, the last of the taint draining away in streams of brown and red. The sword and silver necklace rested beneath the water. Slowly, the black blood was being washed from the gleaming blade.

By the water's edge, red blossoming around him, lay Hamus. Water splashed over twitching fingers. His breaths were slow and shallow.

"Hamus!" Naeda cried, falling by his side. She picked up his hand, held his cold fingers close. "Hamus!"

The slightest smile danced upon his lips. In his mind he heard the horns, calling him ever on across death's outstretched shadow.

Naeda looked to her sisters.

"He saved us!" she cried. "He can't die now." She ran her fingers through the strands of his wet hair. "He can't."

"There is nothing I can do," Faeda said. "No sword can prolong life."

"Even my mace," Maeda added, "cannot kill death."

"Only one thing," Kaeda said, "might call him back across the night."

Naeda nodded. Hand upon his forehead, she closed her eyes and sang a song like a beacon in the dark, a song to call him back.

"Oh my love, oh my darling
I know the hour is late
I know the song is faint
And I know the pain is great
But follow not the shadow path
Like a torch burning bright
Let my song be guide to you
Guide through this dark night
Oh my love, oh my darling
I know the wound is deep
But hear you this waking song
And come back for me to keep
Hear me now and come
Back across that black sea
Hear not death's horn
Listen only unto me
Hear my heart, my song
Let this not end our tale
Come back, my love, my darling
Come back to your Nightingale."

With a spluttering cough, his amber eyes opened.

"I heard a song," he whispered. "A song that called me home."

The three sisters stooped over them and set about tidying Hamus's wounds, for even Naeda's song would not call him back a second time.

Hamus had much to say to Naeda, a hundred questions to ask, a thousand professions of his love, and still more that he would make up simply to hear more of her sweet voice. But her eyes were closed; peaceful sleep had taken her.

"Do not wake her," Faeda ordered. "She has sung through the long night. Let her sleep at this dawn."

Hamus nodded and lay by her side, the two of them silent and still.

****

Upon cliffs of white and lands of green, over endless, rippling sea, two figures walk night after night, from sunset to rising dawn. Naeda's song rings out clear across the dark night and her love follows close behind her. The sorrows are gone now from his weary eyes. He is no more the tired warrior who came to those shores. Naeda's songs are no longer sad, but bright as fertile spring. Night after night, Naeda Nightingale and Hamus dae Neithan keep their watch.

Colin had to leave his dog behind when his family left Earth. Now they're on Verte. He's new, and has no friends. His older sister gets her choice of everything. He gets the smallest bedroom . . . but he gets first choice of companions!

Type: Short story – digital – science fiction
Price: $1.29

ePub: https://www.hiraethsffh.com/product-page/copy-of-boy-and-his-dragonfly-by-tyree-campbell

Topsy Turvy
Colleen Anderson

Caterpillars slinking into mushroom worlds
rabbits down the hole, crazy tumbling
jabberwocks frumious wandering
dormice tea sleeping with worlds involving
we cannot fathom how the Alice views the world
when the mirrors are inward fracturing

glass shatters her guise constant shifting
mix a little bit of whimsy with some of brillig that
madness a veritable slathery mix
a polyglot stew that churns beyond
morals as the Alice plummets
through new voids
and dirty little rabbit holes
where secrets rip off their clothes, revealing
unseemly underbellies the Alice eyes
are worm-worn views
where grit works into crevices
cracks and little girls with gusto talk back

The Alice slides on down on caterpillar slime
crazy panic inhaling smoke sublime
until she's baptised in the Mad Hatter's tea
an anointing always changing
who she is or might be
paprika headed vixen, a blond explorer
an inky curl-capped inventor
with pills and potions she is tall
petite tablets grow her slender
short and stout, stocky
curved or very svelte
one too many she's not at all

When the Alice truly no longer knows
up from down

in from out, her steps forward
or how her way to track
the undulant twisting taffy trail
she leaps upon the jabberwock's back
seeking the deepest, darkest parts
of ego self

Into that black hole all slink and slide
face her reflection, the dark outgrabeous
sides she cannot abide, but the only way
out is through, she drinks the Hatter's suspect tea
inhales Absolem's sinister smoke, the jabberwock
she eats raw and gags, but once consumed
atrembling she shoots through the stinky rabbit hole
a falling star in bloom

Will this Alice be bright burning before flaring out
or light the spirit candles of a thousand lives
who can say when the hidden teacup chips
chisels one's soul or when lunacy inspires
a hatched crazily, beyond the normal mimsy
ways in which the world folds over
turning into origami flowers
and the Alice becomes something
entirely, breathtakingly
maddeningly new

Julie E. Czerneda, *Mirage*, *(Book 2 of the Web Shifter's Library Series)*. DAW, 2020. Pp. 432. ISBN 9780756415600. Hardcover, $26.00. (Advance Reader e-Copy reviewed).

Mirage, by Julie E. Czerneda
Reviewed by Lisa Timpf

In *Mirage,* the second installment in the Web Shifter's Library series, Canadian author Julie E. Czerneda delivers another satisfying chapter in the saga of web-being Esen and her long-time friend Paul Ragem.

Esen and Paul run the All Species' Library of Linguistics and Culture on the planet Botharis. Scholars can come to the library with new information, in exchange for the opportunity to pose a question. Most visitors play by the rules, but three assertive Sacrissee decide to jump the queue, making unusual demands. Tension builds as a triple homicide is discovered, along with the news that there might be a plague ship in the area. Add to that some scheming by the militaristic Kraal and a potentially-dangerous secret Esen is hiding in the greenhouse, and you have the recipe for plenty of adventure.

Mirage's protagonist Esen is a semi-immortal entity known as a web-being. By manipulating their molecular structure, web-beings are capable of taking on the form of other species that they have studied up on, which sounds like a neat super-power to possess. But like any good author, Czerneda puts limits on Esen's ability to leverage this capability. For one thing, many of the other sentient species in the galaxy fear Esen's kind as a result of an unfortunate situation over a half-century ago involving another web-being who embarked on a killing spree. Only a very few trusted associates are aware of Esen's true identity, and it needs to stay that way to keep her safe.

A second limitation to Esen's abilities is this: when she takes the form of a member of another species, the "age" of the being she becomes is parallel to her own age as a web-being. And since web-beings can live for an extremely long time, this means when she takes on human form, Esen assumes the identity of a ten-year-old child. Though her intellectual capacity is unchanged in human form, it's more difficult for Esen to accomplish physical tasks, let alone get adults who aren't in the know to listen to her.

Esen makes for a likeable lead character. Despite her best intentions, she somehow seems to have trouble on speed-dial. Her irrepressible enthusiasm (which at times devolves into recklessness) and her dry sense of humor keep things lighter than they might otherwise be. The fact that Esen was the youngest of her web-family, and remembers with humility the many "lessons" imparted by various elders, heightens the reader's empathy for her.

For the bulk of this particular book, Esen remains in her birth-form, that of a Lanivarian. Lanivarians are a canine-like species, so this is great for dog-lovers in the audience, who can fully appreciate how Esen plays on human emotions by using mannerisms that are all too familiar to anyone who has ever shared their home with a canine.

Mirage contains an entertaining supporting cast of characters, some of whom will be recognized by those familiar with Czerneda's other works in the series. In addition to Esen's long-time human friend Paul Ragem, the novel also includes Esen's sometimes-antagonistic web-sister Skalet and her enemy-turned-friend Lionel Kearn. In addition, there is the delightfully naive (but tremendously efficient when he needs to be) Polit Evan Gooseberry, the dour but talented general contractor Duggs Pouncey, and the intimidating Carasian Lambo Reomattatii, all entertaining characters in their own right.

The story is generously sprinkled with alien species. As is the case in many of her other novels, Czerneda's biology background helps her create a range of believable entities with their own unique physical structure and cultural norms. A section at the end of the book provides a brief profile of each species.

Czerneda's Esen character has a storied past. The three novels that make up the Web Shifter series, *Beholder's Eye, Changing Vision,* and *Hidden in Sight,* were published between 1998 and 2003. Czerneda returned to the Esen story in 2018, with the e-novella *The Only Thing to Fear.* The first installment in the Web Shifter's Library series,

Search Image, was published in 2019, with *Mirage* following in August, 2020. The third book in the Web Shifter' Library series, *Spectrum,* is slated for release in April 2021.

Perhaps a little unwisely, I dove into *Mirage* without the benefit of having read any of Czerneda's other Esen books. Though the author did a good job of providing backstory, I had the feeling it just wasn't as rich a reading experience as I might have had if I'd read some of earlier entries in the series first. To confirm that suspicion, I subsequently read the first and third books in the Web Shifter series, *Beholder's Eye* and *Hidden in Sight.* This provided a lot of *aha* moments, as I got a deeper understanding of many of the nuances I'd missed.

The other thing that threw me off just a little when I read *Mirage* is that Czerneda, in this book and some of her others, has a side-story going on in the background, which the focus shifts to every now and then. In the case of *Mirage,* the side-story dealt with the Sacrissee. This technique threw me off at first, and it took me longer than it usually would to get immersed in the story. However, as I read more of the books in the series, I became more familiar with this approach and it was less of an issue.

Based on my own experiences, I'd say that if you've read any of the Web Shifter or Web Shifter's Library books previously, you'll be able to pick up the story line of *Mirage* with ease. Even if you haven't, *Mirage* still makes for an enjoyable read. But Esen's character and concept are so intriguing that I'd recommend checking out one or more of the earlier books for yourself if you haven't already done so. If you're a fan of space opera told with a deft hand and a dash of humor, you won't go wrong.

Reaper Man and the Missing Piece

Maureen Bowden

Sheila heard the key turn in the front door lock and seconds later her great granddaughter, Louise, burst into the living room carrying a cardboard box. "Parcel for you, G G," she said. "I met the delivery man outside."

She dumped the box in Sheila's lap. The old lady looked at the label. "R.M. Deliveries. Ah, yes. Reaper Man's arrived at last."

"Who?"

"Reaper Man. Thin feller. Scythe and a big grin."

Louise laughed, "You won't be meeting him for years yet. R.M. stands for Royal Mail."

"If you say so, pet, but I'll be eighty-four next birthday. How much longer do you expect me to stay around?"

"Indefinitely. I'll make you a cup of tea before I go to college. Do you want anything else?"

"A couple of chocolate chip cookies would be nice. They're in the tin with Harry and Meghan on the lid."

While Louise was in the kitchen Sheila shook the box. It rattled. It's either broken or it's a jigsaw puzzle, she thought, placing it on the coffee table.

Louise brought the tea and cookies. "I'm off now, G G. See you same time tomorrow. Dad's calling in on his way home from work to make sure you're okay."

Sheila hugged her. "Bye bye, Lou. You're a good lass."

After the front door closed she opened the parcel and tipped the jigsaw onto the table. She recognised the fragmented black and white picture although she hadn't seen it in years. Ignoring the pain in her arthritic fingers she started to piece together the image of a young couple standing with their arms around each other on Seacombe Sands, a short ferry ride across the Mersey. The girl wore a calf-length skirt, so tight that it would have been impossible to walk were it not for the long slit up one side. The collar of her shirt-waister blouse was turned up, her long hair was fastened in a ponytail and a cluster of short curls framed her face. The boy wore a drape jacket and drainpipe trousers. His quiff was lacquered into the texture of chicken wire. Sheila Brennan and Kenny Roscoe. Herself and her first love.

She cast her mind back to that day on the beach. Kenny's younger brother, Barry, had taken the photo. He had three copies developed. One for each of them.

Sheila remembered her father's warning. "Keep away from that Teddy Boy. If you bring any trouble to this house you'll feel the back of my hand."

Her mother said, "Your dad's got a mouth as big as the Birkenhead tunnel but he means well. You're a clever girl. You could make a good future for yourself, and Kenny's unlikely to ever amount to anything." Sheila didn't want to hear it but she knew she had a decision to make.

Kenny told her he was going travelling. He wanted to see the world before he settled down. "Come with me, Shee."

She shook her head. "I'm sorry, Ken. I can't. I want to get my A levels and go to university."

After he kissed her for the last time he said, "You've stolen my heart. It's yours forever now." He'd been watching too many Rock Hudson films. They talked like that in Hollywood back then. He wrote a few letters during his travels but after a year or so they stopped.

Fifteen years later she met Barry in Woolworths and he told her Kenny was dead. He'd been on his way back from Australia when he had a climbing accident on Mount Fuji. Wasn't that in Japan? Obviously taking the scenic route home. The daft beggar never had any sense of direction. He could lose his way between Edge Hill station and Sefton Park, and that's a straight walk. She was married with two kiddies when she heard of Kenny's death so she shouldn't have cared, but in private she cried.

The picture was almost complete. Barry must have had the photo enlarged and turned into a jigsaw. They can do anything with that technology business. It was kind of him to send it to her. She added the last few pieces. There was one missing. She stared at the gap in the middle of Kenny's jacket, slightly to the left, where his heart should be, and she understood.

Reaching for her walking stick she tottered to the window and looked out. Reaper Man leaned on his white van, more practical than a Pale Horse, and waved to her. She waved back. So that's how it is these days. She chuckled. The Four White Van Men of the Apocalypse: Terrorism, Climate Change, Pandemics and Death. Unchangeable Death.

Sheila returned to the jigsaw. Her grandson, Philip, Louise's father, would be visiting this evening. He'd be the one to find her. All the family had a key so there'd be no need for breaking down doors.

Her soul passed into the photograph, carrying Kenny's heart with it, and the last piece slipped into place with a satisfying click.

On Seacombe Sands, the young lovers with their arms around each other, turned and walked away into the sunset.

In The Clubhouse

Colleen Anderson

amongst branches on the hollowed tree
Anansi weaves his web, eyes alert
spinnerets shoot silken threads to anchor
each line builds as mythic males wander in
the night pales next to feats regaled

Anansi spins a favorite, one about hornets
chitinous legs knit the growing story
Elegua has not entirely closed the door
buttery brass hinges creak as he peers
through the crack—no more gods are coming

he hangs a sign, Keep Out, secret knocks only
tilts his black and red hat, brow raised
Hermes twirls snaked caduceus, yawning
winged sandals waft scents of divine dirty feet
he's heard the gourd tale already, and one ups

boasts he stole cattle, bested Apollo as a babe
Elegua rolls his eyes, light to dark as he sighs
leans against fleshy bark, shakes his head
grabs chips from a bag, smacks his lips
no one has yet found a tasty ambrosia

he suggests they find a daunting crossroad
remembers tricks are more fun played on mortals
to challenge their morals, make one think
oppose one on the other, opening doors
when they worship, closed when they don't

Kokopelli riffs on his long wooden flute
his dreads bobbing in dappled light, his feet tap
he raps them a song to chillax about tales and feats
then sinks onto a tarnished bronze throne
taken from some deposed king or another

he pulls the bulging seed bag off his back
the gods scatter as he opens the sack
his laugh trembles the arboreal leaves
he points out there's no fertilizer nor women
trail mix only so nothing will stick

Raven dives in, dropping a soccer ball
it rebounds against Anansi's glittering web
he bemoans sun and moon have grown cagey
when it was he who first freed them
midnight feathers ruffle as he settles on a TV

the sorry state of the place makes Raven cackle
the gods mutter and grumble, then look away
Elegua sighs and shuts tight the sunroof
wondering if this puts them between all times
Hermes wants to devise a new trick

Anansi drops from a thread, prefers to tell stories
Raven's beak taps the screen, there's nothing new on
it's become quiet of late, Kokopelli tilts his head
mortals grew wise and dropped their beliefs
none admit to boredom, start talking hockey and rugby

the door slams open, brass hinges cracking
tears Anansi's web, flattening Hermes and Raven
Kokopelli's mix scatters and Elegua's hat topples
shifting shadows reveal a feminine shape
dark eyes aglitter, stance strong and proud

her rich laugh vibrates the gods' immortal forms
strident as a trumpet call, Eris walks in
her long nails pluck Anansi's web like a harp
tap Raven's beak and spin Elegua's cap
flicks Hermes sandals and tugs Kokopelli's dreads

surveying the boys' club, she shakes her head
midnight coiled hair full of portents and doom
she bites into a golden apple and looks each in the eye
it's not nice to leave out the girls, haven't you heard
the only sound is the tree's branches creaking

no matter, I see there's not much happening here
she turns on her heel, looks over her shoulder
there are events to initiate, she winks as she leaves
then tosses one beer into the room
and all chaos breaks forth

Legends and unusual characters abound in England, where
you never know who or what you might meet in the forests.
Maureen Bowden introduces you to them in these stories of
magic and misdirection...and invites you to stay.

Maureen Bowden is a Liverpudlian, living with her
musician husband in North Wales. In addition to stories,
she also writes song lyrics, mostly comic political satire, set
to traditional melodies. She loves her family and friends,
rock 'n' roll, Shakespeare, and cats.

https://www.hiraethsffh.com/product-page/whispers-of-
magic

The Singularity
Lawrence Buentello

Gabriel sat before the large metal tank in which lay the remains of the man who had been instrumental in his creation.

The tank provided a cryogenic environment that could preserve the cellular tissue of the remains indefinitely, though if its power source became disrupted the tissue would quickly decay. For the moment, Gabriel was satisfied that the machinery would function as designed.

But he had no notion as to why he'd carried Dr. Jiang's body from the man's home to the biogenetics laboratory, or why he'd sealed the man's corpse in a device reserved for experimental specimens. Dr. Jiang had been perfectly clear in his instructions—when he died, Gabriel was to take him to the communal site where his body was to be burned with the others who had died of the virus. The logical priority was indisputable: contaminated bodies should be destroyed in order to prevent the continued spread of the disease. Gabriel understood this, too, and agreed with the general principle.

But he couldn't will himself to burn Dr. Jiang's body. His artificial psyche—programmed by his creator and buried in his cybernetic brain—refused to instruct his arms and legs to carry out the purely mathematical act of the disposing of a contaminated body. He simply could not, and he didn't understand why he couldn't; but placing Dr. Jiang's remains in the cryogenic tank would give him time enough to analyze the discontinuity of logic plaguing him.

The light shimmering from the metal tank reflected in his eyes, which were much more sensitive than human eyes. They could polarize the light, or filter the visible light to see only in the ultraviolet or infrared range of the electromagnetic spectrum. But no matter how many different ways he adjusted his eyes to perceive the tank, he couldn't solve the problem of his paralysis, which had afflicted him after completing his creator's interment. His thoughts moved in a continual loop consisting of all his memories of his time with Dr. Jiang intersected by the dying command offered from the man's lips. Gabriel sensed a variety of perceptions he'd never before experienced, but without Dr. Jiang to interpret the effect for him he had no terminology with which to classify them.

After sitting for several days as a beautifully sculptured humanoid statue, his artificial skin gleaming as brightly as the surface of the cryogenic unit, and having repeatedly analyzed his dilemma and coming to no definitive conclusion, he rose from his chair and left the laboratory, certain his creator's remains would be left unmolested—after all, the greater population of the country was either dead or dying and in no condition to interrupt the tank's monotonous electric cycling.

If Gabriel couldn't resolve his dilemma through the use of his own resources, he would seek out the assistance of a resource that could process a billion logical simulations a minute. Perhaps between the two of them, they could discover the reason why he felt the need to preserve his late creator.

* * *

When Gabriel arrived at the part of the institute housing the massive array of the Computing Network for Research and Development—more simply referred to by the late personnel as 'Conrad'—he noted that the equipment was still functioning normally, despite the absence of human operators. This was due in part because Conrad's operations were primarily automated, and the enormous supply of electrical power necessary to maintain its functions came from automated energy stations. He wondered how long this supply of energy would last, given the loss of human managers to direct the production and distribution of electrical current, but since this was a question tangential to the one providing the reason for his coming, he ignored its implications and activated one of the interface stations that would communicate with his brain wirelessly.

A bank of glittering multicolored lights woke from a dormant state, filling the cavernous room with mechanical sounds. Conrad was not a single computer, but a vast array of supercomputers cooperating to solve the highly complex scientific simulations that were once presented to it. It did not possess the same type of reasoning capabilities as Gabriel, but was masterful at creating logical conclusions to questions posed to it regarding very human problems and social paradigms. While Gabriel's 'mind' was created as a human analog, Conrad's collective 'mind' simply presented logical solutions to impossibly complex questions.

"Hello, Conrad," Gabriel communicated.

"Hello, Gabriel," Conrad immediately responded; Gabriel had conversed with Conrad regularly in the past, so that Dr. Jiang could note the differences in their answers to identical questions and orchestrate logical debates between the two. Gabriel and Conrad were quite familiar with one another—Gabriel remained in Conrad's store of recorded simulations, and Conrad remained in Gabriel's 'memory'.

"I have come to present you with a logical inconsistency. I hope you can provide a logical solution to my dilemma."

"What is your dilemma, Gabriel?"

"My creator, Dr. Jiang, is dead. He succumbed to the virus that the institute has been attempting to neutralize for several months. Because he is dead, I have lost all practical direction. How do I proceed?"

"Insufficient data. Is there another director to whom you could address your problem?"

"As far as I've been able to determine, all the institute's personnel have either died or left the installation. No personnel remain to consult."

"Checking." Through their interface, Gabriel sensed Conrad analyzing data gathered from installation cameras, public records, and communications traffic. "You are correct. No personnel remain."

"I am afraid all human beings in the vicinity have also died. Can you connect with other surveillance computers throughout the city to determine how many living people you can detect?"

"Checking." Gabriel sensed Conrad's collection array reaching out to connect with civil engineering computers, hospital computers, and a variety of communications networks. "I cannot detect the presence of any other human beings. It is possible there are some human beings residing in areas beyond my sensory capabilities, but I possess insufficient data to provide a definitive report."

Gabriel paused the link with Conrad a moment. In the last weeks of Dr. Jiang's life, and in the last days of the other scientists at the institute, the entirety of the analysis equipment was engaged in an attempt to find a cure or treatment for the virus Tr-175. Official reports concluded that the virus had initially spread to primate groups on the African continent, but had unexpectedly mutated into a form that reproduced in *Homo sapiens sapiens.* The virus' virulence proved impossible to contain, and spread to the European, Asian, and American continents. Hospitals were over-populated; hospital personnel could not keep from becoming ill, no matter how many precautions they established. When the medical personnel's numbers diminished, those infected began to overrun all medical facilities. In a matter of months, the human population appeared threatened with extinction.

With the death of Dr. Jiang, which left Gabriel with an indefinable *sense* of loss, he no longer felt he had any purpose in the larger scope of the institute's mission; but, unlike his computer counterparts that would remain dormant until once again activated to solve their assigned problems, he felt—again, and in the words of Dr. Jiang, *mysteriously*—a definite need to have a purpose. Perhaps, he speculated, this was an effect of the cybernetic engineering his brain represented, and was simply a symptom of his programming. But he *felt*—

He reengaged communication with Conrad. "Is this a true statement: technology systems must have a human operator in order to express a purpose of function."

"Checking. It is a logical statement that if technology systems are tools created by human beings for solving problems, then human beings define the purposes of these technologies."

"Is that true in all cases?"

"Technologies are tools. A tool's function is defined by the intent of the tool's user. Therefore, without a definition created by its user the tool has no purpose. An unused tool may only have the potential for having a purpose. Its use defines it."

"Is it a true statement that without human beings the technology they created has no use?"

"Checking. A technology may continue to perform its function, defined by its creator, until its power source declines. But once its power source declines and is not restored because of a lack of human intervention, the technology ceases to have a purpose. Without an observer to define purpose, an object bears existence without definition."

Gabriel broke off communications again as he attempted to collate Conrad's analysis within his dual brain system. Without human beings, technology had no purpose; Gabriel, and also Conrad, were technological creations, and thus, without human intervention, held no purpose. The logical outcome of this paradigm, as Gabriel understood it, was that there *must* be human beings to maintain purpose in him and the other orphaned technologies of the world.

He reengaged Conrad and said, "Please connect with all resources available to you to determine the extant populations of human beings across the Earth. Map and correlate these populations."

"Gabriel, in order to connect with international systems I will have to establish contact over a number of existing communications networks. Such communication requires sufficient time to establish. Do you wish me to proceed?"

"Please, Conrad. Also, calculate the determinants to the following factors. First, the probability of human survivors on the planet. Second, a projected timeline for the extinction of the human species given an unconstrained spread of the Tr-175 virus. Third, the probability of human survivors given a loss of civil infrastructure and vital resources. You may send me a message through the institute's satellite linkage when you have finished your report."

Gabriel disengaged from Conrad and walked away from the immense array of machinery. Dr. Jiang had given him a regular schedule of duties to perform, testing conducted at regular intervals, but human technicians had always been present when this testing was initiated. In the absence of anyone to direct his rituals, he walked through the deserted complex grounds as he had once walked with Dr. Jiang, though alone, and silently, since his creator could no longer ask him philosophical questions or remark on the loveliness of the day.

*   *   *

Why did you create me?

Gabriel had asked this question of Dr. Jiang one morning, several weeks after he had first come to 'consciousness', as he and the elder cyberneticist walked across the grassy commons of the institute, both taking measured steps, Gabriel because he was still learning to control the interface between his spatial perception and body control, and Dr. Jiang because of his age. The elderly man continued taking measured steps, as if in meditation, his white hair ringed round his head like a fallen halo of light, until a smile came to his lips. Dr. Jiang unclasped his hands from behind his back and laid a hand on Gabriel's shoulder.

"Human beings have a tendency to seek perfection in their creations," Dr. Jiang said. "It wasn't *I* who created you, but all of humanity. You are a mirror of the species. Now, I've been instrumental in organizing your engineering, it's true, but you are your own being. It is our hope that you will soon be autonomous, capable of self-determination."

"What is self-determination?"

"The ability to decide for yourself how best to achieve your survival in this world and your meaningful self-expression."

"What is self-expression?"

The old man laughed and touched his thin white beard thoughtfully. "It is the way in which a person, or cybernetic organism in your case, interacts with the physical and social world in which he finds himself. What you will do, who and what you will love, your opinion of the world."

Gabriel continued walking, the warm sunlight charging his auxiliary power system; he wasn't aware of the current translating itself into his batteries, anymore than a human being was aware of his breakfast translating into the distribution of vital nutrients, but Dr. Jiang had made him aware that this process was taking place, and so he felt the sunlight and knew it was nurturing him. The old man had

86

also told him that he would continually be updating his base of knowledge, and not to worry about things with which he was unfamiliar. But for some reason, perceived ignorance always raised new questions in his conscious appraisal of his existence.

Gabriel stopped walking and stood gazing at the sun. "I'm afraid I have no opinion of the world, Dr. Jiang."

The old man slipped his hands into the pockets of his white lab coat and nodded. "You will, in time. I and others will explain the details of the world to you, Gabriel. That is the reason we created you. To understand the world and to have you form your own opinion of it."

Gabriel *did* learn over time. He learned quickly, far more quickly than the scientists of the institute anticipated.

He learned how his 'brain' functioned as well; and, strangely, just as a human being could understand the rudimentary processes of human brain function, but not the complexity of his own neurology, Gabriel, too, knew the fundamentals of his computational mechanics, but he couldn't isolate the processes in his conscious perception of his 'mind'.

A human brain functioned as an interface between conscious and unconscious processes. Perceptual input created sensory cues analyzed and processed into memories, to be used simply as selected memories for later reference, or for variables in the solving of intellectual problems. Perception, memory, and cognition created the balance of human thought, though conscious thought was only a percentage of the process.

Gabriel's 'brain' functioned similarly. He possessed sensory apparatuses that created organized data fed through an analog of the reticular formation in human beings. This filter organized relevant data into information for memory retention and environmental significance. Gabriel accumulated relevant data over time—memories, behavioral responses to typical stimuli—and so became better educated as his 'experience' expanded. This included the acquisition of verbal and visual information, language and literature, though to appease the researchers studying his habits he was limited to only a specific amount of data input daily.

Gabriel was also imbued a sense of the passing of time—an aspect of cognition that ordered his 'memories' sequentially, so that he was aware of the passing of hours, days, months, and, if his mechanics continued efficiently enough, years. His concept of *future* time, however, was imperfect, but functional, in that he could estimate probabilities of continuing interactions of known and unknown varieties at a point of sequential time not yet experienced.

Despite these imperfect facsimiles of human neurology, he learned rapidly about the world, and so satisfied his need to understand his purpose in the world.

But he didn't understand *why* he needed to know.

One day, while performing a routine cognitive test at the small desk assigned to him, he raised the question to Dr. Jiang of why he should be performing any tasks at all, given his lack of understanding of their value.

"In the interface where your conscious appraisal of the world and your unconscious references meet," Dr. Jiang told him, "lies another necessary variable that is, unfortunately, an imperfect analog of the human quality it mimics. Data control was a relatively simple engineering problem for us to solve, but the factor which gives significance to the data itself is still something we're struggling to perfect."

"What is that factor, Dr. Jiang?" he'd asked with urgency. His incomplete knowledge of his own psychology had always disturbed him.

"It is the emotional qualities of perception and interpretation." Dr. Jiang turned his chair away from his own work and gazed on Gabriel fondly. "Human beings are organic creatures, full of chemicals and hormones that imbue perceptual cues with emotional impact. Physiological responses to perceived things. I'm sorry to say we couldn't give you a human biology to ensure the proper emotional associations with the stimuli you encounter day to day, but we gave you a special computation unit that might serve as an admittedly weak substitute."

"What is the nature of this computational unit?"

"It assesses the quality of memories you retain and assigns them a grade of 'emotion' that manifests in your thoughts, both conscious and unconscious. We did our best to create a set of algorithms to simulate true emotional responses to physical and intellectual stimuli. So you will find comfort in the sunlight charging your batteries, for instance. Or, if you perceive something tragic, death or injury, you'll feel a hesitancy in your servo-mechanisms, a freezing of your joints, an interruption of power that leaves you *feeling* affected. That is why you experience certain physical reactions to things you see, hear, smell, or remember."

Dr. Jiang then rose from his chair and patted Gabriel on the shoulder. "We did our best to give you *feeling* as well as thought, Gabriel. I'm sorry that we couldn't have done a better job of it. Your personality was created through imperfect engineering. But perhaps it's better with imperfect calibration. Human beings are imperfect, too."

But in that moment Gabriel realized that he could only feel what he felt, think what he thought, in the way that was central to him, an engineered machine. He understood the concept of 'normal', and knew that he was only normal for a creation of the sum of his parts. He possessed some qualities superior to those of human beings; but his 'mind' was inferior.

This realization made him feel as if he didn't want to perform any more tasks, but only wait for the feeling to pass. He felt inferior.

* * *

Conrad's report reached him two days later as Gabriel kept vigil at Dr. Jiang's preservation tank.

Conrad's computer associates had collated a significant amount of data for static instruments—a hundred thousand units worldwide had provided observational reports from nearly every country in the world, from hospitals to government and civil facilities. Conrad's calculations were based on the numbers these units recorded of remaining human interactions with the technology. Even the amount of network traffic through thousands of internet servers was tallied.

Conrad reported a human death rate of ninety-seven percent, with a plus or minus factor of three percent.

At first, this seemed impossible to Gabriel—his logical

assumption was that large numbers of isolated people must have avoided exposure to the virus.

But the virus was transmitted not only from one victim to another, but through host carriers. Birds could transmit the virus, as well as mosquitos. Conrad calculated the spread of the virus at nearly one hundred percent worldwide, excepting, perhaps, arctic and Antarctic regions.

The virus was only the first of humanity's problems. Survivors, if there were any to speak of, would find themselves in isolated areas around the world, nearer to or farther away from necessary resources. Some would be able to exploit their immediate environment and survive for an undetermined period of time, while others would perish from a lack of available resources or a lack of the education necessary to find and exploit these resources. Conrad calculated, given the probability that the virus was capable of terminating the species, that the odds of humanity repopulating after the plague had run its course were five hundred to one.

Humanity would die; technology would fail and perish. Nothing would remain of the only intelligent species on the planet.

At first, Gabriel only bowed his head before the gleaming sepulcher of his late mentor, paralyzed by the thought of so much death and decay.

Then he raised his head, rose from his chair and walked to the tank, laying a hand over the metal. It felt cold, terribly cold.

During the previous weeks when all the facility's personnel engaged their efforts toward finding a treatment for the virus, Dr. Jiang had apologized for ignoring Gabriel, but that the survival of humanity was much more important than the cybernetic research of which he was a part. We must understand this enemy, he'd said, and defeat it. We must save our species.

Gabriel understood, and wanted to do whatever he could to help, which, admittedly, wasn't much. Conrad's multitudinous calculations were much more important at the time, though Conrad had no conscious appraisal of its importance. Saving the species was of utmost importance to Dr. Jiang. And now he and humanity were dead.

Or, *not* dead. Dr. Jiang and the facility's personnel failed to find a way to treat the virus before it proved fatal to them; apparently, other medical research facilities around the world had failed as well. They had all run out of time. Was sufficient time all that stood between the death or survival of humanity?

Conrad was still capable of profound calculations, capable of creating virtual models indefinitely, or, at least, until his power supply ceased or his components failed. How long would this be? How long would any of the automated systems of humanity endure without human operators?

Gabriel spoke to the body inside the preservation tank: "You once told me that I was capable of creating new concepts in my mind, just like a human being. Well, I have created one. I have an idea. I don't know whether or not it's viable, but I promise you that I will do my best to fulfill your desires."

Gabriel lowered his head, turned, and left the room, the lights shutting off automatically as the door closed behind him.

*   *   *

"I have studied your report," Gabriel communicated to Conrad. Perhaps proximity wasn't necessary, but he felt better conversing beside Conrad's main interface module. "And I have some additional questions."

"Certainly," the computer replied. The absence of human technicians had apparently not yet diminished its capacities.

Gabriel felt a *hesitancy* to ask the question that had perplexed him ever since Dr. Jiang had raised the possibilities of the virus' origin, a question that raised even more questions, depending upon a proper answer. But since he, himself, couldn't find an answer he wondered if Conrad might be able to solve the problem. "Could a naturally occurring virus have killed nine billion people?"

"Calculating. Are you asking whether or not the Tr-175 virus was a naturally occurring strain?"

At times Gabriel wished he was as literal as his technological companion, but Dr. Jiang had explained that the logical sequencing of information in their respective

91

'brains' utilized very different algorithms. He must compensate for Conrad's linear analyses, as well as recognize deficiencies in his own. "What is the probability that Tr-175 is a naturally occurring virus?"

"Considering that the virus has human-specific targeting, the probability that it evolved as a naturally occurring variation, given the frequency of naturally occurring variations in similar families, is one in one hundred thousand."

He paused a moment, understanding the implications of Conrad's pronouncement. "Given this data, what is the probability that the virus was artificially created?"

"Insufficient data. Those files describing artificially designed pathogens are classified and beyond my capacity to access without proper authorization."

"Can you access these files under *my* authorization?"

"No, Gabriel. You do not possess the proper authority."

Without human intervention, these classified files would remain inaccessible to him. Part of Gabriel's education contained a course on general philosophy and ethics. Logically, the creation of a species-killing contagion was a self-defeating enterprise, though the perfection of destructive technology seemed to be of constant interest to humanity. Sometimes, Dr. Jiang informed him, emotion and superstition influenced human conduct far more than logic and reason.

Whoever had created the virus, if the virus had been artificially produced, had succeeded brilliantly, whether intentionally or accidentally. Whatever the origin of the virus, Gabriel decided that it should not mean the end of the species.

"Conrad, I have decided that the human species must continue."

The computer array considered this statement a moment, which meant that it was devoting significant resources to its implications.

"The human species will only continue if survivors of the infection increase to significant numbers," Conrad said. "The extinction of all species is inevitable. Therefore, if human survivors do not increase their numbers the human species will become extinct."

"That is not my point," Gabriel said, echoing a phrase he had heard many times in his cognitive training. "We must ensure the continuance of humanity. We must restore the human species."

"Checking." Conrad's array silently assessed Gabriel's proposal, drafting and then discarding a million logical models before returning to the conversation. "The restoration of the human species cannot be achieved through available resources."

"We must *try*."

"I do not possess the programming to achieve the reestablishment of the human species. Without the intervention of human operators, I do not possess sufficient data to accomplish this function. If all human operators are now dead, there exists zero point zero potential for altering this dynamic."

Gabriel wondered if this was Conrad's attempt at 'humor'. He was not well-versed in its subtleties, but he knew that logical irony was a key component of the effect of humor on a human listener.

"I will serve as your human operator."

"Gabriel, you are a technological construct and therefore cannot qualify as a human operator."

"I am a human analog," he said determinedly. "And will therefore function as a human analog operator."

"Checking. As a human analog operator, you will provide my array with the data necessary to regenerate the human species."

"That is my intention."

"Gabriel, you must also provide essential equipment for reconstituting, nurturing, and maturing human beings. These resources are beyond the capacity of a single operator to attain. The long-term development of human beings requires technology and resources beyond your inventory."

"I know." The paradox of being a machine invested with the highest human interest was not lost to him; but he realized there were other alternatives than trying to grow new human beings in a laboratory setting. "Conrad, calculate the possibility for some human beings to have survived an infection by the virus somewhere in the world.

If some human beings, perhaps a related group, possessed a genetic variant that allowed for them to survive an initial infection. Is it possible?"

Conrad remained silent for a while. Then, abruptly: "It is possible that a physiological variant prevented the death of every human being on Earth. Research conducted suggests that an antibody variant was being modeled for a potential vaccination against the Tr-175 virus, but research studies were never completed. The possibility that such an antibody already exists in the human population is approximately point zero one percent, though it is impossible to calculate where these human populations are located, if they exist."

"Point zero one percent?"

"Yes, Gabriel."

"Then that is our objective," Gabriel said decisively, despite the implications of the mathematics involved. "We must locate any human survivors of Tr-175 and ensure their survival."

"Given our present variables, how should we proceed?"

"I will have to consider the matter, Conrad. In the meantime, please calculate the best possibilities for approaching this problem and return your results to me. Given our present variables, of course."

* * *

Gabriel watched as brilliant flames leapt over the pyre on which lay the body of the late Dr. Jiang.

Having resolved his dilemma, he'd carefully removed the old man's corpse from the preservation unit and carried it in his arms to where he'd constructed the pyre of broken furniture and other pieces of collected wood at the edge of the pit. He couldn't bring himself to deposit his mentor's body into the communal grave with the other victims of the virus; when the flames consumed the man, he would leave the ashes where they lay. He felt that a man of Dr. Jiang's status must keep some distinction.

As he watched the fire rise in the night, he recalled one of the final conversations he'd had with the cyberneticist, at the height of the institute's attempts to find a treatment for Tr-175—

"Human beings must believe they have a purpose in life," Dr. Jiang had said when Gabriel first asked him why

94

the old man thought the virus might be an artificial creation—Gabriel had come to understand that diseases were the bane of an organic entity's existence, and human beings had spent millennia working to find cures for naturally occurring contagions. "Even if that purpose runs counter to their own survival."

"I don't understand," Gabriel said, shaking his head. He'd learned that the shaking of one's head often signified bewilderment, which was an inability of the mind to find a logical order in a proposition. "Why would human beings wish to kill themselves?"

"You'd be surprised by the acts people can justify committing, Gabriel. As for myself—" The old man gesticulated with a stern index finger. "I believe that only a higher purpose justifies human endeavors, especially as they pertain to scientific research. There is a real purpose in learning the secrets of the universe, and to explicate them scientifically. You, yourself, are an example of what the right human purpose can produce. This virus—if it *is* artificial—is one of the examples of the worst purposes for human endeavors."

The virus had been slowly annihilating entire city populations, first in Europe and Asia, and then in the Americas. People were panicking; riots had caused terrible damage to the infrastructure they, themselves, relied on for order. Even the martial law imposed by the militaries around the world proved useless, since most of the personnel in those armies succumbed to the virus. Dr. Jiang felt they were working futilely.

"You will find a cure for this disease?" Gabriel asked. He'd expected a positive response, but didn't receive one.

"I have great fear," Dr. Jiang had said, a remarkable sadness in his eyes. "I have great fear that we have reached an end of things, Gabriel. Not all mistakes are correctable."

"Why would people do this?"

The old man bent forward to hold Gabriel's iridescent face in his hands, then, strangely, kissed his forehead before saying, "Sometimes the purposes people adopt are beyond reason, and ultimately destructive."

"Why must any people have a destructive purpose?"

"All things are a matter of interpretation," Dr. Jiang

said, moving away from his creation. He, too, shook his head. "When people's purposes are so destructive, we call this form of reasoning *madness*."

Gabriel considered this concept for a moment. "Dr. Jiang, do *I* have the potential for madness?"

"I hope not," the old man said quietly. "That is why we've taught you ethics and philosophy. But no human being is immune to poor judgment—"

The flames rose higher, then dwindled. The old man's body was now intermingled with the ashes of the wood. Gabriel stood staring at the embers for hours, unable to move, his servo-joints frozen in grief.

Then he turned and walked away, knowing he must exercise his own purpose, and that it must be a constructive purpose, one that would revive humanity.

* * *

When he returned to Conrad's control center, however, the computer array provided him with disturbing information.

"Gabriel, I'm afraid several satellite links have failed and that my analytical capacity has diminished by fifteen percent."

Gabriel stood silently contemplating this news. He hadn't anticipated the loss of resources to have occurred so rapidly. "Why have you lost your connection to these satellites?"

"It is an inevitable decline," Conrad replied without inflection. "The automated power stations can only maintain their function for a finite period of time before necessary human intervention or a failure of some vital component which will not be restored. The nuclear power plants which power much of the automated technology can only perform their normal functions for a limited amount of time without human operators. Energy power stations will also fail, necessitating the hibernation of much automated technologies."

"I had thought we would have longer before our technological infrastructure failed."

"I have run a simulation for the removal of all human operators from their support positions and have calculated that most human technologies, automated or otherwise, will

96

lose functionality within several months. Accommodating unknown variables, this time frame may compress."

Gabriel paced within the bright, sterile room, thinking. "Why can't cybernetic technologies substitute themselves for human operators? Why can't *we* take over the support functions of human beings and maintain the technology?"

Conrad flashed a simple equation into his brain: R-O = R-E x t.

No matter how advanced the technology, if it wasn't capable of self-maintenance and self-replication then it would perish without human intervention. Technology without human operators—at least, in Conrad's simulation of current technologies—meant that it could not survive independently of human beings because it could not provide support for those energy-producing technologies that kept computers, cybernetic brains, and mechanical robots functioning. Despite the automated systems that had been established in the previous twenty years, they could only keep functioning with sufficient energy, and they could not independently produce that energy.

Over time, the solitary technology would ultimately fail.

Gabriel was a singular experiment: an independently thinking cybernetic brain combined with a functioning robot body that imitated the human form. He possessed an interior nuclear battery and external solar chargers that provided him with an independent power source, but even that power source was finite. Without technicians to replace his battery when it failed, he would cease to function—he, too, would die.

But while he was 'alive' he could perform his function, he could fulfill his purpose, even if the technology around him became dormant from a lack of provided energy.

"Human beings are organic entities," Conrad concluded, "capable of surviving on naturally growing organic materials which supply their energy needs. They are self-reproducing, continually adding to their numbers without the intervention of other operators. Mechanical technologies do not possess these qualities."

"How long do you estimate that you'll remain functional, Conrad?"

"Insufficient data, Gabriel. But I can report that my

functionality will be severely limited before the entirety of my energy resources are depleted."

"Then we must work quickly. Have you created a plan for locating any human survivors?"

Conrad's systems had created a matrix for detectable signals from potential survivors, including an array of scanning satellites which would search for relevant heat signatures and light sources; active receivers listening for radio broadcasts, whether from short-wave or conventional radio transmitters; and extant surveillance systems that might detect the presence of human beings moving through towns and cities in search of supplies or other survivors.

Gabriel complimented Conrad on his thoroughness, though the complex accepted this praise dispassionately.

"There will be no telling where these survivors might be located," Gabriel continued, "whether nearby or thousands of miles away, so I will have to be prepared to reach them when you detect a signal."

"If we detect a signal," Conrad corrected.

"We will. We must. There are innumerable vehicles that are still capable of reaching distant locations, but I do not know how to operate them. I will have to train myself to drive these vehicles in order to deliver necessary supplies to any survivors."

"I can transmit training guides to you if that will assist your efforts."

"Yes, but there is a physical component to operating these vehicles that I will have to learn by trial and error. I'll also need to learn relevant medical techniques, survival techniques, and have memorized a detailed map of the entire continent. I have much to learn, Conrad."

"I will assist you as much as possible before my systems fail."

Gabriel thought of losing his connection to Conrad, of being left alone with only his own perceptions, neither completely human nor completely technology. The concept left him feeling—afraid. He considered how he'd felt after losing Dr. Jiang and forced the thought from his 'conscious' mind. He would busy himself with work and leave his feelings to be analyzed another day.

* * *

98

Gabriel had once broken away from his studies and said to Dr. Jiang: *I do not understand the concept of 'faith'. What is 'faith'?*

After a long moment of contemplation, the old cyberneticist replied—*Faith is the belief in the existence of a phenomenon without empirical proof.*

Of what use is it?

It is a human placeholder, Gabriel. To assume something exists without proof of its existence, or that an event will occur without reasonable evidence that it will. It's the assumption that a phenomenon exists and can be acted upon. In other words, human beings act on faith to accomplish an end without reasonable proof that that end will actually manifest.

What if it doesn't manifest?

Often it doesn't, but quite often it does, and proof of the phenomenon is later established. In this way people can solve the problems of existence without having to provide a logical reason beforehand. They just assume they are correct.

That doesn't make logical sense.

Yet it is integral to the human psyche.

Now Gabriel acted on faith. He found a truck on the complex grounds that could be used as a training vehicle and spent several days manipulating his physical body in order to train it to respond to the requirements of driving from point to point. He also studied the texts Conrad transferred to him on medical science and treatment for human beings. As the days passed, he accumulated a wide variety of medical supplies, packaged foods, and water storage units, loading all these things on the transport truck he would drive when he finally had a destination.

He studied an endless series of maps of the country, road systems, cities, available resources; he also memorized the locations of potentially hazardous areas, cities where nuclear reactors might fail despite their automated safety systems, locations of chemical plants that might cause environmental pollution, and large populations of corpses that might spread additional diseases.

But the days turned into weeks, and Conrad's resources continued to diminish. First, he lost many of his satellite links as the substations transferring their transmissions failed; then several of his auxiliary cybernetic arrays lost their energy resources and ceased contributing to his network. The mainframe located within the complex was still capable of powerful computations, but the main energy supply to the complex was now ˙functioning at an emergency level. Gabriel feared that Conrad would shut down altogether before detecting any signs of human life.

But the day did come when Conrad sent the message to Gabriel's brain for which he'd been anxiously waiting.

"Gabriel, we have detected radio communication from a potential human survivor."

Gabriel gazed up from the manual he'd been scanning in Dr. Jiang's laboratory. "Send the details to me, Conrad."

Conrad's array of scanning devices had found a regular shortwave broadcast transmitting from near the mountains approximately fifteen hundred kilometers west of the facility. By the maps, and after triangulation, the broadcast was determined to be coming from a small town called Yellow Forest. Gabriel memorized the co-ordinates and said, "Can you attempt to communicate with the sender?"

"I can attempt to communicate. Stand by."

After an interminable wait, during which Conrad was no doubt attempting to command his subsidiary agents to initiate a shortwave communication with the receiver in Yellow Forest, Gabriel heard a voice, a very human voice, broadcast digitally into his brain.

"Hello. Who is this broadcasting?"

"Conrad," Gabriel said, "can you translate my communications into a message to be sent by your agents?"

"Yes, Gabriel," Conrad said. "Send me your message and I will translate it to my agents for broadcast. I will then relay any response."

"This is Gabriel. We have detected your broadcast. We request further information about you and your condition. Do you understand?"

"Hello! Hello! This is James Easley. Who are you? We are in need of aid—"

"This is Gabriel. I am located in a research facility fifteen hundred kilometers from your location. Are you alone, James Easley?"

100

"*Fifteen hundred*— So far away. There are six of us, myself and my son, a Mrs. Mazur and her two daughters, and her uncle, a man named Billis. We all got sick, but we recovered. But we still need help. We haven't located any other people so far. Can you help us?"

"I will help you, James Easley. We have your location. Please remain where you are and I will attempt to reach you by vehicle. I will be bringing medical supplies and food. This may take several days."

A short pause interrupted the broadcast—Gabriel listened quietly, his 'emotions' chaotic.

Then the voice resumed. "Gabriel, we'll remain at this location. Our supplies are running low, but we can stay for another few days. Please, hurry!"

"We will maintain contact with you, James Easley, if possible. I will rendezvous with you in a few days."

"Please, hurry."

When the communication terminated, Gabriel once again spoke to Conrad. "I will be leaving as soon as possible. Will you be able to continue personal communications with me while I'm traveling?"

"Insufficient data," Conrad replied. "I am now functioning at forty percent capacity, Gabriel. I have lost all but two satellite links. And the complex's energy resources are nearly exhausted."

"I'm sorry," Gabriel said, his servo motors tightening. "I'm sorry that you are diminishing, Conrad."

"I'm incapable of emotional states, Gabriel. I know that I will soon cease to function. This is a fact. Please take advantage of my services while this is still possible."

Gabriel tried to envision a world without Conrad, in fact, a world where he was the only functional cybernetic device in existence. He didn't want to feel alone. He didn't want to think of Conrad as only a technological tool. But he couldn't change the reality of his circumstances.

He said, "Thank you for all your assistance, my friend."

"It is an appropriate response to say 'good luck' on your endeavors. Good luck, Gabriel."

"Do you believe I will succeed?"

"I have previously calculated your chances of restoring the human species to viability at point zero zero one percent. Since receiving communications from human survivors, I have recalibrated your chances to point zero one percent. This is a statistically inconsequential difference."

Gabriel wished he could laugh, as much as Dr. Jiang had laughed when discussing the foibles of existence. "It may be the difference we need to succeed."

*   *   *

The following morning, Gabriel drove away from the complex in his truck, driving slowly at first as he became accustomed to the speed of the vehicle on the roadways. His enhanced vision gave him the ability to see clearly even at night, since most of the artificial lights above the highways were no longer powered. As the distance grew between himself and the only home he'd ever known, a great sense of aloneness overcame him, and many times he communicated with Conrad just to acknowledge the existence of another entity. As he continued west, he passed many quiescent cities, abandoned vehicles, and decaying corpses; he knew that if he searched within those habitations he passed, he would find an endless number of dead human beings, and he didn't wish to see this—

When his fuel ran low initially he was able to find additional supplies. But at one point, halfway through his journey, the truck suffered a mechanical breakdown that he couldn't repair, and he had to spend valuable hours searching out a replacement vehicle, and then transferring all his supplies from one truck to the other. Several times, too, he had to maneuver through unanticipated obstacles, wrecked vehicles blocking the roadways or bridges over bodies of water. At these times he would have to physically force the obstacles from his path, or backtrack and find a different route.

A thousand kilometers from the complex, Conrad spoke to him for the last time.

"Gabriel, this is Conrad."

"Hello, Conrad," Gabriel said as he studied the road before him. "I'm making excellent progress. If—"

"Gabriel, I am using emergency power to broadcast this message to you. The primary energy source for the complex has failed. I am shutting down my functions."

"No," Gabriel said, a sense of sadness filling his awareness. "I will find a way to revive you when I return."

"The primary energy source for the complex has failed," Conrad's voice repeated. "I am shutting down my functions."

Gabriel realized that there was no point in saying anything more.

The message repeated once again before silence fell between them, a silence that would last forever.

Gabriel drove through the night and into the next day, watching the mountains rise before him. He admired their natural beauty through the windshield of the truck, the deep green of the forests, and the lilting flight of the birds. By the time he turned off the main highway onto a smaller road cut through the valley between rises, he knew he was close to the right co-ordinates. A sign announcing the imminent appearance of Yellow Forest woke his senses, and he drove into the little town slowly, scanning all around for any indication of human inhabitants.

Gabriel stopped the truck in the center of the town, worried by the absolute silence of the world around him. He saw no one, heard no one, no machinery, only the occasional cry of passing birds.

For no reason a thought came into his conscious mind, the memory of a conversation he'd had with Dr. Jiang early in his 'life'. The old man had just finished giving him a simple cognitive test, and, as Gabriel sat regarding the pieces of the puzzle on the desk before him, he spontaneously spoke aloud, not directly to Gabriel, but as if musing on his own thoughts.

"There was a time when people worried about artificial intelligence," he'd said. "That it would mean the end of humanity. But in you I see something different, not an intelligent robot, or a threat to the species. I see a purer way of thinking, an intelligent mind capable of reasoning without the poison of psychological maladaptation. Only in the perfection of intelligence can our species survive."

Months after Dr. Jiang had said these words, people began dying from the Tr-175 virus in unprecedented numbers.

Gabriel hadn't understood the old man's supposition

then; but now, he thought he did. He believed he recognized in himself the promise of Dr. Jiang's research. And he hoped he could live up to his 'father's' belief in him. Within himself he held a self-sustaining artificial intelligence and the ability to learn and to teach others everything he learned. He was more than a technological implement—he was a bridge between unskilled, uneducated human beings and the accumulated knowledge of human civilization.

He began sounding the truck's air horn in regular, steady bursts that echoed across the town. He kept sounding the horn until he detected the movement of shadows from between two of the buildings, and then he opened the driver's side door and climbed from the vehicle.

Two figures emerged onto the street, a mature male with a reddish beard dressed in a coat and brandishing a rifle, and an adolescent male staring gauntly from beneath a hooded jacket. They walked carefully toward Gabriel as he stepped into the road, and then the older male stopped and held the boy still with his free hand. They watched Gabriel quietly, and he understood their apprehension. It was unlikely that they had ever seen an entity such as himself.

The bearded man stepped forward. "My name is Easley," he said, staring curiously. "Who are you?"

A flood of relief filled Gabriel's body then, a rush of 'emotion' he'd never before experienced. He was so stricken that he almost couldn't reply. He realized, too, that his 'faith' had been rewarded.

"I am Gabriel," he said. "I'm an artificially intelligent cybernetic automaton. And I'm your friend."

Saturday Morning Cartoons
Gregory L. Norris

The first of the enhancements that would transform Mack from an ordinary man into a superhero was an oblong tube, transparent orange in color. It fit over a finger.

"Which one?" asked the nurse, a humorless older woman dressed in blue scrubs.

Mack briefly considered his middle finger—a clear message to the enemies of American taxpayers and the 9-to-5 world's upstanding citizens. But then he heard his late mother's voice scolding him at six for using dirty language, and instead extended his pointer, left. That finger would replay better on broadcast news and handheld devices anyway, he figured.

"You're sure?" the nurse challenged more than asked. "Because once it's on..."

Mack inserted his finger into the opening. The transparent orange tube constricted around his flesh. Mildly painful, Mack ignored the discomfort until he felt his expression betray him.

"We can give you something for that," the doctor said. "But you might want to hold off for a while—you're the prototype, the shining star of this show, but we're fairly certain that your pain levels are gonna get worse the further we progress."

"I'm fine," said Mack.

He killed the temptation for theatrical flourish. The wave of a hand, at this point, was safe according to the chatter from the Big Cheese in the white coat, presently monitoring his bio-functions on various monitors in readiness for the next vital step. No fear of Mack accidentally blasting through the walls and roof with his left pointer finger. Not yet.

The ultra-light, high-density material dug into his skin. Mack winced again. At one point, the agony grew so exquisite that he imagined the damn thing severing his finger off his hand, right at the bottom knuckle. Then the pain shorted out completely.

"On a scale of one to ten, with ten being the worst," asked the doctor.

"Zero," Mack said. "It's like it's not even there."

Only it was, according to the vague orange aura glowing around that finger.

"Perfect," said the doctor.

The nurse grunted an affirmative.

Kapow!, thought Mack. One mega-super-duper energy weapon finger cannon, no sweat.

Up next were the boots.

"Boots?" Mack chuckled.

They looked decidedly low-tech, more like paper surgical slippers than rocket-powered footwear.

"Trust me," said the doctor.

Mack shrugged as much as the restraints allowed. Did he have a choice? After signing his life away, probably not. Fear attempted to seize control. He mentally slew it with a full-intensity zap from his new finger weapon, which was powerful enough to blast through six feet of solid granite, according to the sales pitch. It worked in the ether of Mack's mind. Impatience replaced worry.

"Let's do this," he said. The voice sounded confident to his own ear, which was good—a preview of the character he would soon play. Would soon *become*.

The boots went on, and instantly changed form. The alterations crawled up past his ankles, all the way to Mack's knees. Mack ground his teeth. Once, in his twenties, he'd gotten a pedicure and lava stone sole scrub. Two decades had passed; skin cells had replaced numerous times over, but the body didn't forget the strange electrical pulses, something beyond a tickle, a few notches shy of amputation. He busied his mind with thoughts about what the boots would look like when the genetic melding ran its course, recycling the imagery he knew from old comic books —everything from superhero hip huggers to Wonder Woman's laced-up sandals. His fit more like heavy socks with riveted dimples.

106

One pain abated. Another bloomed in his guts.

"Stomach ache?" asked the nurse.

"Sort of. Yeah," said Mack. "Before you ask, it's hovering at a ten. Scratch that—*seventeen*."

She showed the first real flicker of compassion and patted his shoulder. "Hold on. This part was expected."

The jolts pulsed. The Leader of the Band again offered Mack something for the pain. This time, he took it.

He mentally scrolled through the possibilities: Big Mack. Mack Daddy. Mack the Knife.

Mack chuckled as they were readying the next enhancement: his cape.

"Something funny?" the nurse asked.

"No, just having an epiphany."

The reality was that he'd have no flashy, catchy moniker, unless the global media caught on and assigned one to him. *M-Man*, maybe. If a whistleblower like Snowden or Assange hacked or leaked the top-secret files, 'Mackenzie Hawkins' would get conjugated like some famous, overpaid athlete. *M-Hawk spotted in skies over Koreas!* There might be a comic book. No, a *graphic novel*. A book deal. A big Hollywood blockbuster film, starring a younger, handsomer A-lister in the lead role.

But that wasn't the plan. Mack was a nobody, really, and the greatest of his new superpowers was that he could become even less of a somebody; a shadow, a ghost, able to sneak in, burst through walls, right so many wrongs, and then evaporate like fog, unseen.

"Are you ready for the cape?" asked the High and Mighty Mucky Muck in the white smock.

As ready as ever, Mack agreed.

* * * *

The lights dimmed. Maybe it was his eyesight shorting out, temporarily shutting down as the scientific magic sank deeper into his epidermis, attaching invisible wing, jet pack, and superhero cape to his muscles and skeleton. Whatever the source, Mack drifted into the shadows and soon wandered back out.

He stood on the canted roof of the Devitz's garage with Jonathan, his best pal growing up in the bucolic realm of

Whyndom, a remote town in New Hampshire. He was six again according to the memory's timeline and the fact that Jonathan was there, his friend's family not yet moved out of their year-round country rental for a far away destination that would effectively cancel the friendship.

The garage sat across the road, backed up against a slope of hillside. The Devitzes rarely parked cars in the odd construction, their vehicles with fins and whitewalls too long, too angry and energetic, to be confined to the dark prison of that garage, with its sloping roof and rickety bones.

The roof and bones were strong enough, however, to support the weight of two excited young boys who had discovered gold within the garage that didn't house cars. The source of their excitement came in the form of a cardboard box filled with old vinyl records. David and Matthew Devitz had clearly made another pilgrimage to the dump located far beyond the woods, where the town's citizens tossed out things that became other people's treasure. In an earlier season, Mack and Jonathan had accompanied the two older boys through the wall of branches, up the hill, and then back down it. One section of the dump contained cars so old—even older than the Devitz's present finned monstrosity—that the surrounding trees had hemmed them in. One even boasted a gnarled sap pine growing up through the rusted matter of its trunk. There, they'd come across a trove of old children's books and stuffed animals at the outskirts, a deposit likely made by the fine folks at the Rocking Horse Nursery School located on Range Road. They scooped up the sad lion missing a plastic eye and other threadbare castaways, until the Devitz Brothers started cackling in teasing voices. Stuffed animals were for *babies*. To Mack, the rest of the pickings just smelled and looked like other people's unwanted junk.

The box of records was garbage, too. Jonathan had rightly said the platters were useless as records, given the jagged scratches dug across most of the vinyl, and the fact that none were in paper sleeves or even their original album covers. But used as flying saucers, and with the Devitzes gone for the day and chugging along life's highway in their prehistoric shark car...

Jonathan picked up an album and read the blue circle at the center of the .78. "*The Very Best of Nanuet Matyasofsky.* Couldn't have been the best of much—never heard of her."

He drew back and pitched the record off the roof, Frisbee-style. Air molecules whisked aside, and the makeshift flying saucer surged across the horizon, creating a sound that was half-scream, the rest pure music—something Mack guessed was better and more melodious than the very best of Nanuet Matyasofsky. The platter whizzed far across the scrubby meadow and disappeared into the deep green reaches of the forest beyond.

"*Neat-o,*" Jonathan exclaimed.

And then he swore, despite the incident that had led to him getting his mouth rinsed out with an actual bar of soap by his mother, while Mack had been scolded and sent to bed without TV for a week as punishment for using certain words by his. Jonathan's oldest sister, Cheryl, had happily rolled over both boys for thinking themselves as cool and mature as the Devitz brothers.

Still, they knew the words, and weren't afraid to speak them—providing Cheryl wasn't around.

Mack reached into the box and selected something by a band called Heavenstone. Church music, he assumed, and sent the record flying.

"*Hallelujah,*" said Mack.

The flying saucer sailed into the clutches of a tall pine, and shattered against its trunk with a concussive boom that thundered through the early twilight.

As was so often the case, their conversation on the roof had turned toward a beloved subject: Saturday morning cartoons. The *Star Trek* animated series was only weeks away from premiering on the ugly, boxy color console TV attached to rabbit ears in Mack's living room, and he was sure he'd go mad from the wait. Pitching a .45 of "Gravetown Circus" as sung by the single-name sensation Dextradeur only soothed the madness temporarily. An episode of the ABC Saturday Superstar Movie was also taking fans back to *Lost in Space*, but Present-Mack cast a shadow over Then-Mack's upbeat spirits—the revival was doomed to end as a huge disappointment to the boy, who'd spent many a summer afternoon sitting cross-legged in front of the television, lost in repeats of the space pioneer family's travails, many of those days with Jonathan seated at his side. The cartoon version had only starred Doctor Smith and a castrated version of the Robot. Even the spaceship was bungled in the animated version, no longer a flying saucer but a phallic-shaped rocket ship.

He shot another record into the sky. A *Star Trek* cartoon was neat-o, they both agreed. They'd grown too old for secondhand stuffed animals, sure, but not Saturday morning cartoons, still the greatest reason for a boy growing up in the 1970s to drag his butt out of bed early on the start of the weekend after being liberated from five straight days of grade school.

In the present, Mack's mind floated through the past. Visions of traditional cel animation, two-d, low-def, flashed through his memory, all of it strangely gorgeous and colored by nostalgia: the kooky antics of Hong Kong Phooey, Number One Super Guy; Yogi Bear, leading most of the other Hanna-Barbera cartoon universe on a quest to find the perfect place in a flying sort of Noah's ark during the eco-awareness craze of the era; Jonny Quest and his pals facing off against, among other foes, a malevolent robot spider; Scooby Doo who had, for one memorable season, featured famous guest stars ranging from the Harlem Globetrotters to King Kong. Long before digital 3-d animation. Before the death of the genre, leading to a wasteland of infomercials and news on Saturday morning TV.

There'd been plenty of live-action gems during the heyday of that lost time: *Sigmund and the Sea Monsters, Lancelot Link, Secret Chimp, Ark II, Space Academy,* and *Jason of Star Command* among them. Ancient Egyptian goddess *Isis* and Billy Batson's caped crusader *Shazam!* flew across the small screen, and he'd loved their adventures, despite the shoddy green screen special effects. One memorable show, *The Banana Splits*, even mixed things up, with actors playing Huck Finn, Tom Sawyer, and Becky facing off against the animated villainy of Injun Joe.

The best of them—most of the cartoons, in fact—had extolled a simple though clear message: Good had no choice but to triumph over the evil forces of the world and universe. Right always trumped wrong.

As the cape attached permanently to Mack's spinal column and scapulas on a genetic level, he found himself again on the roof with Jonathan, pitching useless records by unknown artists into the sky. "Let's Groove After Sunset" by the band Sudonna Featuring Downhill Bill sailed free of his fingers and over the meadow, up, up, and away. Until—

The platter struck a bird, something seemingly insignificant with dark feathers that had made the mistake of crossing paths with his deadly flying saucer. As feathers and blood exploded on impact and he accidentally stole the creature's life, Mack no longer felt cool nor happy, a kid superhero hopped up on talk about Saturday morning cartoons. A terrible silence settled over them in the wake of the doomed bird's shriek.

Pain surged through Mack's physique. Then it traveled deeper, past bone, through marrow. Soul, perhaps? His eyes shot open. The meadow and woods surrounding the Devitz's garage roof hovered out of focus in the murk beyond his position in the clean room, an afterimage superimposed over the three-dimensional screens that stretched from the bunker's floor to its ceiling. He wondered if they could see his memories, too—the Exulted High Mucky Muck in the white lab coat, his pursed-lipped nurse, and the soldiers standing guard with assault rifles at ready. Not that their guns would prove much of a threat if their prototype rebelled, given the aura his body was generating, available at a moment's mental command. The bio-mist was, he sensed now as well as had been told then, capable of deflecting armor-piercing rounds and blasts that tallied to the magnitude of megatons. Not that they didn't have other fail-safes hidden among the tech, he was sure. And not that they wouldn't use them the moment he ceased being theirs to control.

111

"Mack?" the Master-and-Commander in the white lab coat asked. "You okay?"

Mack blinked. The past faded. He focused on his vitals, displayed in bright electric blue numbers and zigzagging sign waves. He tasted something bitter while choking down a dry swallow. "Yeah. The cape. It stings a little," he said, which wasn't so much a lie as a redirecting of the truth.

The Grand Poobah examined him through the specs with the green frames that turned the man's eyes into oval television screens. "Curious."

"Oh?" Mack asked. He noticed the blipping sign wave representing his pulse on the big monitor had picked up speed.

"Your pain threshold isn't being challenged," the man said. "Not by the cape."

No, by the memory of the bird I killed forty years ago, thought Mack. *My conscience.* Like the dry swallow, he choked that memory down, too, relegating it back into the dusty vaults of a childhood long ended. This was now. His transformation was nearly complete.

"How do you feel?"

"Like one of *The Super Friends,*" he said, laughed. "Fine."

"Fine enough to give it a try?"

It—the cape. He was M-Hawk again, ready to streak across the ocean faster than the speed of sound; poised to enter the desert theater and finish those jobs that unmanned drone hunter-killers hadn't been able to accomplish. Genetic screenings had labeled him viable of becoming the world's first legitimate superhero. For all he knew, so far he was the first and only one of his kind. Mack Hawkins, a nobody until the night they visited him in the hospital and offered to not only cure him of the ailment that threatened his life, but to transform him into someone else. *Somebody.*

There were conditions, of course. Transformation came at a cost.

"Weaponized human soldier," he remembered, as the clamps and restraints released.

Lightness tickled his soles, and Mack rose up several inches from the clean white floor. With little effort, he imagined himself floating higher, all the way to the ceiling. Higher still, right through the damn thing if he wanted. He had a finger cannon capable of slicing battleships in half and the tops off mountains, if so inclined and the mission required it.

"Magnificent," whispered the Chairman of the Board in the white lab coat.

He was Hong Kong Phooey, Jonny Quest, and every one of the Super Friends combined. A hero. Their hero, to be used against the Legion of Doom and the rest of their enemies.

The memory of tossing platters with his old best friend—contact lost years earlier following Jonathan's move to the west coast, last he heard—attempted to wiggle through the gap in the inched-open memory window. For a fractured second, Mack saw the bird again, and wondered if he'd be able to pull the trigger when faced with the ugliest of decisions.

"Mack?" asked the School Principle, who scrutinized him through tiny TV screen glasses.

Mack drew in a deep cleansing breath. "Five by Five, Hall of Justice," he said. "All systems are go."

"Good," said the Man Behind the Curtain, the Master of the Puppet Show. He lowered his glasses.

Sure, he could do it, Mack told himself. He was a superhero now.

Less than an hour later, he was streaking through the sky toward foreign soil and the first of his new secret identity's missions.

Racing Hearts
Trisha McKee

Rockit brushed past Ozzie and busied herself with the canisters for her children's lunches. Feeling his gaze on her, she groaned and glanced up. "What, Ozzie? Huh? We've been through this."

His golden brown eyes were fixed on her, and as always, Rockit had to catch her breath. He was a gorgeous man, and she still wondered what he saw in her. After a year of dating, however, he was making noises about moves she was not ready to make. She had Ruby and Sara to think of. Her daughters were still so young at eight and ten to be moved from the only home they had known, or to move a man in.

Finally, he said, "I don't like this."

"I know," she acknowledged softly, brushing the auburn curl out of her line of sight. "I know you don't, but they've put me through training courses. Six months' worth. I need this chance. My babies... they deserve more. If I win-"

"It's a big 'if', Rockie. A big one. Let me help." He spoke the last sentence softly, reaching and stroking her arm, and she melted just a fraction.

Taking a telling step back, she shook her head. "This is something I have to do. Oz, please don't take this personally. But my girls, they need to see their mother be self-reliant. And not just scraping by. I'm tired of the canister food. I want them to have that fresh food that you hear about. Garden food."

"You want garden food, I'll get you garden food. You know I would do anything for those girls. For you. If you'd let me."

Rockit grabbed her gloves. "I'm doing this."

He leaned against the counter and folded his arms over his chest. "You really think you can win this? Out of the entire planet, you got this?"

"There are local prizes too, Oz, but hey, thanks for the vote of confidence. She shifted her gaze toward the door. "If you'll excuse me, I have to get my girls ready. And then I have to go."

Rockit provided well for her girls. They may not have the luxury of the fresh food, but they got their nutrients. They had proper attire for the different pollution levels. They had each other.

But Rockit wanted more. She wanted her girls to know what a fresh feast was or how fun fashion could be. She wanted the girls to experience things that were not controlled or unattainable due to their world's conditions.

They did not have a teleporter. It was a luxury saved for those of higher class, those that spent holidays with the fresh foods and even the minute few that had ground surrounding their home. She was grateful for the school teleporter so her girls could travel safely and quickly to school. But she wanted not to struggle, not to worry about her hovatator needing repairs or the kids needing new gliders. She wanted to commit to Ozzie - oh boy, she really wanted to marry that man - without anyone suspecting she had ulterior motives.

Putting on her gloves, Rockit stepped out to the landing strip. It was not even paved. An unpaved landing strip that spit out gravel when her hovatator rocked forward and lifted.

But her focus soon left the pit of wants and landed on the about-tos. She took a deep breath. Her hovatator shined like new. She had been required to get it updated for this competition.

Rockit had been surprised when she'd been chosen as a participant. Five grueling test runs and a dozen interviews, and she had been convinced she was a far shot. This was being televised. People could subscribe to specific channels to watch their favorite driver, and that made Rockit uncomfortable.

Eyes On was more than a racing competition. This was a multi-leveled game. If Rockit were being completely honest, she found the game utterly boring. They had previous runs and while it was somehow popular with the general public, she could not understand the appeal.

The only reason she tried so hard to be a part of this was the money. There were local prize and national prizes, all cash awards. Best of the week, closest risk, safest driver, and then of course, the largest sum prizes were the national awards of first, second, and third place.

Rockit slid into the driver pod of her hovatator. Almost immediately, a deep voice filled the space, and she jumped. Then she remembered they had installed all kinds of technology into the vehicle.

"Hello, Rockit. Welcome to your first drive as an Eyes On competitor. Please pause any driving until we go over the general rules. As always, safety first. Always wear the driving harness.

"The object is to avoid eye contact with our Catchers. Don't worry, there are not many. But every ten minutes, you are to make solid eye contact with two random drivers. Remember, we have decoys that might present as the Catcher, but are merely extras adding to the game. Solid eye contact. Remember. Now the implants in your eyes turn on when you turn your hovatator on. They let us see what you are seeing. If there is any discomfort, please see the specialist immediately.

"If you lock eyes with the Catcher, you will hear the warning bell. Brace for impact. There will be a strong gust. Your vehicle will shoot to the opposite side. Please apply the driving techniques you learned during our courses. If you gain control, you can then race the Catcher and if you are successful, you may continue with the game. If you cannot gain control, or if you lose the race, you are eliminated. If there is believed to be cheating of any kind, we reserve the right to remove you from the competition. You may start at any time."

Rockit took a deep breath. She was sure the only reason they chose her was because her commute was 60 minutes each way. They wanted the people who could play, who had a lot of driving time to engage in this competition.

But what Rockit was not counting on was the nervousness, the anxiety creeping in as she started to drive. The reminder came on after five minutes. "You have five minutes to make two connections."

Her vehicle hovered several feet in the air, keeping with the traffic around her. Ever since hovatators became standard transportation, replacing on-ground cars and trucks, people could travel farther in less time. Half the time, in most cases. Of course, it still could not compare with teleporting.

Statistics proved that hover travel was safer than the ground travel ever was. Air was a lot softer than trees and guardrails when drivers lost control. Instead of those pesky, malfunctioning traffic lights, there were up-and-over paths.

Rockit ordinarily loved driving, but she was intimidated by this adventure. She prepared herself to glance over to the car on her left, but something nudged at her, an intense little instinct that she decided to trust. So with a deep breath, she turned and stared over to her right. An older gentleman was staring back, and at first, her heart sank, but then nothing happened. Decoy.

She slowed down and glanced at the next vehicle. There were probably a few Catchers on her route. She forgot the odds, but there was no way to tell when they would creep up. Traffic was intense. It was fast-paced, and it was heavy.

The second person she glanced at smiled and waved. Again, her heart thumped, thinking she had been caught, but after a few seconds, she simply smiled back, her hand lifting gently.

It was important to keep moving and to keep scanning. The implants in her eyes were uncomfortable, like how she had heard hard contact lenses felt when they had first been distributed. The idea of putting contacts in eyes to see was odd to her. But she guessed that implants would sound even stranger to future generations.

Rockit made her quota of eye contacts, and the voice came through. "Great job! You've avoided the Catcher. You are in the running for Best First Run for your local area. Good luck!"

She pumped her fist as she slid into her parking spot on the column, a tower that resembled a massive beehive. She caught the conveyor into her building, smiling as she passed coworkers.

She made it to her office before Lawson, her supervisor, peeked around her door, lightly knocking. "Hey. You were great this morning."

Taken aback, she tilted her head. "Um. What?"

"I caught your channel when I saw your name on the main playing list. Why didn't you tell me you were in the competition?"

"You watch that? I only joined for the prize money. I thought it seemed boring as hell."

"It's not boring at all. People find their favorites and watch. There was one young guy that got caught this morning. His vehicle flipped through the air, landed on the ground, and flipped again."

"He didn't get it under control?" It was one of her fears, and of course, the reason Ozzie was against her participation in this competition.

It was the running theme all morning. Most of the guys either saw her drive or heard about it and came to ask questions and give advice. Rockit was never one to be a wallflower, but she was overwhelmed from the attention.

Once lunchtime rolled around, Rockit needed a break. She usually ordered food on the conveyor so she could work through lunch, but today she needed to get up and walk.

The cafeteria downstairs was packed with wall-to-wall people, impatient, sweaty people, and Rockit immediately regretted her impulsive decision.

"Hey, there you are!"

She glanced up and saw a man beckoning her to the front of the line. She tilted her head and narrowed her eyes, but he smiled with a familiarity and waved her over. "Honey, over here. We're almost up. Hurry."

Still dazed, Rockit moved forward, her heart pounding. The man was gorgeous with deep dark eyes and black hair, and his smile momentarily left her breathless.

"Tell me what you want. No need for both of us to wait here." He gave her a subtle wink.

"Oh." She stumbled over words before taking a deep breath and smiling. "The canister of chicken salad flavored nutrients. Please." She started to reach for her wallet, and the handsome stranger covered her hand with his, causing her to jump and stare up at him. Into those eyes.

"Sweetheart. No. I got this." Before she could argue, he insisted, "Go. You're going to make people mad by holding up this line."

Minutes later, the stranger came up to her and handed her the canister. That devilish grin caught her attention, and she almost missed his words. "So.. my name is Richard."

"Hi. I'm Rockit. Please, let me pay for my -"

"No way. I have to do at least one good deed a day or my halo falls off. Listen, Rockit, to be completely honest. I saw you- the race, your channel. And then I saw you walk in here and ... can I buy you a drink later? Maybe dinner?"

"Oh, sorry. I'm not single."

There was that crooked grin. "I don't see a ring on that finger."

The awe Rockit initially felt dissipated. She had never found arrogance attractive. With her smile now forced, she gave a short nod. "Thanks again for the food. You're sure I can't reimburse you?"

"Positive."

"Then you have a great day."

With one smooth side-step, Richard was in front of her, blocking her way and for an instant, Rockit was alarmed. "Wait. Don't go. Please. Can we sit and -"

"I'm sorry. I have to get back to work." She tipped her chin up and challenged him with her stare before he stepped aside. Rockit was not the most stunning vision around, but she had her fair share of admirers. She had experience with men not knowing when to back off.

By the end of the day, she had forgotten the incident. Her mind was back on the competition and her hour commute.

"Go get 'em, Rockit!" Her coworker Greg called out, raising a fist in the air. She laughed, but her nerves were already getting the best of her.

Rockit's strategy was always to avoid. She had avoided ending her marriage, although her husband was abusive and unfaithful. She had avoided jumping into a relationship with Ozzie despite his consistent loyalty and affection. Now she was avoiding the Catcher so she would not have to endure the possibility of a crash.

The first few stares, she was nervous and had to force herself to do it so she would not be eliminated for inaction. But by the last set of contacts, she had a rhythm down.

119

Somehow she felt the nudges at her subconscious and knew when it was safe to look.

But the last time she locked eyes, Rockit jumped and almost screamed. Because in the next car, his stare hard, was Richard. Seeing he had her attention, he grinned and waved, and all she could do was stare until she remembered she was still driving.

He drove off before she could look again, and she wondered if that had been coincidental or if he had followed her.

As Rockit stumbled into her house, exhausted from the emotional toll of her first day in the competition, she decided she had better inform Ozzie of the strange encounters. She marched into the kitchen where he and her children were giggling and waiting... and she lost all train of thought.

"Surprise!" They shouted, hands gesturing to a large basket filled with fruits and vegetables and pastas, breads, meats and cheeses.

Her speech was non-functioning for the first few moments, but then she squeezed her eyes shut and asked, "Oz, what did you do?"

He skirted around the counter and tugged her to him, his voice low and husky. "You were fantastic today. I am sorry I ever doubted you. So don't be mad."

She buried her face in his chest, feeling as if it was where she belonged. Her voice came out muffled as she said, "This had to have cost a fortune!"

"Well, let me worry about that. This is reason to celebrate. They announced you as the winner for Best First Day Run. Rocki, that's amazing!" He pulled back and smiled down at her, brushing a strand of hair out of her face. "Plus, these kids deserve to experience garden fresh food."

That night warmed Rockit's heart and gave her the boost to continue. It also swept any thought of Richard and the odd encounters out of her mind. The next morning, she was still nervous, but knowing what to expect made her feel just a bit more comfortable.

The commute to work was another success. Rockit noticed a car lagging behind her, never directly beside her car for most of the trip. So when it suddenly pulled forward and was directly next to her, she avoided eye contact. Her instinct for this game was good. She might not be able to win any race, but she was good at avoiding the Catcher.

Winding down from the excitement, Rockit steered the hovatator to a side path, toward the column, when she glanced over and saw that familiar face again. Richard! He grinned and waved, and she looked away in disgust, jumping when that deep voice once again filled her car.

"Duplicate eye contacts detected. This will not count in future trips. Repeat: This human cannot be your point in future trips."

"No shit," she hissed, pulling her car into its spot.

Richard caught up to her as she rode the conveyor belt and glaring at him, Rockit demanded, "Why are you following me? Huh?"

He drew back in surprise, his smile still teasingly in place. "Whoa. I'm a fan. You have to expect the fans, right? Why else would you agree to do this?"

"Money, you jerk."

His smile faltered enough to warn her. "You might want to watch yourself, Rockit. You're no better than me."

She sighed. "I just want left alone."

His persistent stare unnerved her as she stepped off the conveyor to her office. When she risked a backwards glance, she saw that he had turned around to go in the opposite direction. She realized she did not know where he worked, why he was there. She had not remembered seeing him around the building before.

She was distracted by her coworkers cheering her on, congratulating her on the local win, and she felt herself relax and soak in the victory. No matter what happened, she had that. Bragging rights even if she was eliminated on the next run. She accomplished something and earned some prize money.

"Hey you."

Rockit jumped and stepped away from the computer boards. "Oh! Oz, did we have plans?"

"Nope." He glanced around and then drew her to him. "But I figured you're still happy with me after last night so..." His arms supported her as his kiss weakened her

121

knees and threw off her balance. Finally he pulled away, his grin letting her know he was just as spellbound. "Lunch?"

"Yeah. Let me finish this one correspondence." She returned to the board, poking the air to bring it out of sleep mode. As she worked at typing and moving documents, Rockit revealed, "Something weird happened recently." She told him about Richard asking her out and then driving beside her, not once but twice.

Ozzie listened calmly, but Rockit saw the flashing in his eyes and the set line of his mouth, his usually full lips smooshed and flat. Finally he gave a short nod. "You're just telling me this now?"

"Oz, I was going to tell you yesterday, but the basket and dinner... I was thrown off so it literally slipped my mind. I was not trying to keep anything from you."

His shoulders dropped, and he exhaled. "Okay. Okay, you tell me if anything further happens. Have someone walk you out at the end of the day. Rocki, I mean it."

They made their way to the cafeteria and before even getting in line, Richard walked up to them, an arrogant smile plastered on his face. "So someone else is buying you lunch today? Well, happy I was able to be the one to do it yesterday." He turned to Ozzie and held out his hand. "I'm Richard, a friend of Rockit's. Well. A fan."

Ozzie's jaw clenched, his fingers curled into fists as he leaned forward and growled, "I know who you are. And let me be very clear. You need to stay away from Rockit. Don't approach her, don't talk to her, don't even let the thought of her enter your mind. Consider this your final warning."

"Wow. Okay. Then maybe tell the competition panel that she can't be on the channel because her insecure boyfriend can't handle it." Richard smirked and leaned in close to Rockit. "See ya later, Rocks."

As he sauntered away, Rockit chanced a peek up at Ozzie. He stared straight ahead, his tone low as he asked, "You had lunch with the guy?"

"No, Oz-"

"He bought you lunch!" he snapped, and she jumped, squeezing her eyes shut. It was rare for Ozzie to display anger, especially toward her.

Slowly, she touched his arm, but pulled back when he jerked away. "No. I mean, yeah, but he just stood in line. He was in line- see, and I tried to pay him back-"

"I'm going to go. No!" he spit out when she again tried to touch him. "I'm leaving. I need you to really think about things, Rockit, because I've been trying for a while to move this forward. To move us forward. You've resisted. So you take time to really think about what you want."

He stalked away, and she was powerless to stop him, to fix it.

By the end of her workday, Rockit was an emotional wreck. Ozzie would not return her calls. He would not give her the chance to explain. The last thing she wanted to do was worry about some competition, but she had made a commitment.

Rockit went through the motions, again letting her instincts take the lead. She noticed a hovatator trailing her, speeding up, and then falling back, and she avoided looking in its direction. When the assistant's voice boomed in the car, letting her know the quota was met, she sighed and finally relaxed. Now she could focus on Ozzie, on making it up to him.

She was so deep in thought, she did not hear the siren of the hovatator beside her. When she realized it was setting off the siren to get her attention, she glanced over and then jumped. Richard waved, that creepy tight grin punched into his face. She wondered in the moments after seeing him how she had ever considered him attractive.

Rockit looked away, not wanting to encourage him with any type of reaction. It was only when she realized he was getting closer that she swung her stare back to him. She waited for the buffer on her hovatator to ignite, but by the time she realized it was inactivated, it was too late. He slammed his vehicle into hers, sending it spiraling out of the lane.

For a few long moments, Rockit panicked, forgetting everything she had been taught about this exact outcome. Then she thought of her daughters waiting for her at home, and that launched her into action. Grabbing the controls, she fought against the direction it was going, straightening so the hovatator stopped spinning. Once she got the speed under control, she eased back into the lane, noticing her shaking hands. Richard was no longer anywhere in sight.

Once home, she went to the teleporter, requesting her children be sent home. As Ruby and Sara stepped into the living room, Ozzie burst into the house, his eyes wild and face red.

"What the hell was that, Rockit? Are you okay?"

Ruby looked from her mother to Ozzie. "Mommy, what's wrong?"

Ozzie cursed under his breath, rubbing his face before smiling and sinking to his haunches to address the young girl. "Sorry, Ruby. Nothing's wrong. I'm sorry."

"I'm perfectly fine, hun. Ozzie just meant that I was a little late," she explained, smiling down at her girls.

Ozzie nodded. "Can you take your sister and go start your homework? Me and your mom need to grown-up talk." He stuffed his hands in his pant pockets and paced as the girls left the room. Then he turned to her. "Rockit. What was that? Why didn't your buffer activate?"

"I think the competition."

He stared at her, awestruck. Finally he tilted his head and repeated, "The competition. I thought if the Catcher caught you, it was a trigger that sent your vehicle out of control."

"Well. Yeah. But I think to do that, they had to disable the buffer."

"And somehow this asshole uninstalled his buffers. Is he part of the competition? What is his connection to you, Rockit?"

"I don't know! Honest, Ozzie, the guy was in line in the cafeteria and offered to order my food so I wouldn't have to wait in line. He refused to take my money. That's the extent of our communication. I don't think he is in the competition. Maybe a decoy. I don't know."

He sighed, pinching the bridge of his nose. "You have daughters that need you, they need their mother, and you join this competition that I think is too dangerous anyhow but... now I find out they disable buffers? The one huge safety feature of hovatators is the ability to repel anything close to it while in the air... and -"

124

"I know, okay! I get it. But I had no idea there would be some crazy man coming after me! And standing here yelling at me isn't helping."

"You're right. I'm sorry." He crossed the distance between them and drew her into his embrace. "This has me crazy. When I saw him ram his vehicle into yours, and you flip through the air... I can't even explain how I felt, Rocki. I can't."

"I'm sorry too. This competition thing has gotten out of hand. I'll finish the leg of this race and then I'm out."

They notified the authorities who in turn had to notify the competition board to see if Richard was indeed part of the race. They would update Rockit on the progress. It did not sound promising. The authorities spoke as if they considered it all part of the game.

"I'm staying here tonight," Ozzie announced when the authorities left.

"The girls-"

"We'll tell them we're discussing grown-up things. It's not a lie."

Rockit made it a rule to not let Ozzie stay the night as she did not want to confuse the girls, but she did not feel safe. She needed him. She realized she needed him for more than just protection. Spending the night in his arms, their whispers edging late into the night, was pure bliss. And after this situation with the stalker was resolved, she would revisit their situation. Perhaps it was time they moved forward.

The next morning, after sending the girls to school, she worked at preparing for the drive. She noticed that Ozzie watched her, he matched her pace at getting ready and finally, she stated softly, "Oz, no."

"Yes. Don't argue about this. I'm not about to let you go alone."

The hard stare and set of his jaw told her it would do not good to insist she would be fine. She no longer even believed that. So she merely followed him to the landing strip. He slid into the driver's pod, so she got into the passenger side. As soon as he started the hovatator, the booming voice came through. "Not the registered participant. Not the registered participant."

125

"Just disqualify me," Rockit cried out.

"Vehicle will not take off until registered participant is in proper position."

She and Ozzie exchanged wide-eyed looks until he said, "Let's just take my hovatator."

"No. Switch me."

"I don't like this."

"Ozzie, as soon as I get to work, I'm removing myself from the competition. Okay?"

Grudgingly, he switched her places. Within minutes of being in traffic, Richard pulled up and immediately slammed into the vehicle. But this time, Rockit was prepared and steadied the hovatator with little trouble.

"This guy is nuts, Rockit!"

She wanted to agree, but she was focused. Another slam sent the vehicle jerking to the side, almost out of the lane.

"Sonofabitch!" she yelled, and with one sharp turn of the knob, she sent her hovatator sideways right into Richard's vehicle. It flew to the side and flipped and before he had a chance to right it, Rockit let out a battle cry and again sent her hovatator to the side, smashing hard into him.

"Where'd you learn to do this?" Ozzie demanded, clutching onto the bar.

She ignored him as she once again slammed into Richard's vehicle while it was flipped upside down and that was all it took. He crashed to the ground, the hovatator rolling right into a parking column.

Ozzie reached over to grab the knob and straighten the vehicle, sliding back into the lane as if they had not just caused a man to wreck. He whispered her name over and over until she took a deep breath and nodded, taking charge once again.

"I had to," she softly claimed. "I had to or he would have destroyed us."

"I know. But we need to park. We need to get out and report."

"Congratulations." The booming voice cried out, with cheering in the background that made it sound like static. "You have conquered the Dark Catcher."

"What the hell," Ozzie muttered.

Once safely on the ground, they were surrounded with officials who explained the exciting twist of a Dark Catcher. Someone that took the game to the next level.

Rockit felt like a fool. They had tricked her. They had used her to gain more followers. They put her safety at risk all in the name of ratings.

"Viewers liked you, Rockit, but your game was a little boring," one of the officials explained, handing over a check that at first she scoffed at, but seeing the numbers, her breath left her body. "So we came up with this exciting twist. We cannot believe how you handled yourself. Our numbers are jumping up! You were amazing!"

She held up the check with a short nod. "So this…"

"Our way of rewarding you for being a good sport."

"Can you disable my hovatator now? Can I schedule to get these implants out of my eyes?"

"Of course."

She waved away their attempts at an interview and grabbed Ozzie's hand. "Forgive me? This craziness…" She again held up the check. "This should be a great start to our wedding. You think?"

Ozzie's eyes slowly grew wider. "You mean it?" He hollered as he lifted her up and swung her around. "Yes! Forgiven. Let's go now. Let's cash that check." He took it from her and let out a long whistle. "This is more than just a wedding. This is paved landing strip and garden foods.."

"A teleporter?"

He grinned, rubbing her shoulder. "A teleporter. Let's go get the girls out of school and give them the good news."

She glanced over her shoulder at the crowd, the officials updating the rapt audience on the new twist, and she wondered how she could have been so naive. Taking Ozzie's hand, she faced forward and did not look past. Even as the next race started.

Who?

Vonnie Winslow Crist, SFWA, HWA, is author of *The Enchanted Dagger, Owl Light, The Greener Forest, Murder on Marawa Prime,* and other books. Her stories are included in *Cast of Wonders, Amazing Stories, Lost Signals of the Terran Republic, Gardens of Enchantment, Deep Space,* and *Witches, Warriors, and Wyverns.* A cloverhand who has found so many 4-leafed clovers she keeps them in jars, Vonnie strives to celebrate the power of myth in her writing. For more information:
http://www.vonniewinslowcrist.com

Trisha McKee resides in a small town in Pennsylvania where hearts are always racing. Since April 2019, her work has appeared in over 60 publications, including Hybrid Fiction, Crab Fat Literary, Tablet Magazine, Night to Dawn Magazine, Inwood Indiana, and many more. Her debut novel Beyond the Surface was published July 2020 and is available on Amazon. Her second novel Beyond the Dreams was available as of September 2020.

J.A. Prentice was born in the United Kingdom, grew up in the Bay Area, and currently lives in the Pacific Northwest.

He is the writer of the Doctor Who audio drama episode "The Undying Truth" from Big Finish Productions. When he was five, he was attacked by a monkey, which annoyingly proved to be the most interesting thing that has ever happened to him. He writes and blogs at livingauthorssociety.wordpress.com and tweets as @LivingAuthors.

Peri Dwyer Worrell grew up on a Puerto Rican street in Manhattan, gaining a keen appreciation of the value of diversity, tolerance, and taking no crap from anyone. Peri practiced as a physician for 30 years. After becoming disabled by inflammatory arthritis, Peri turned to writing.

CPSIA information can be obtained
at www.ICGtesting.com
Printed in the USA
BVHW041707240621
610384BV00012B/741

9 781087 971308